LITTLE
NIGHTMARES,
LITTLE DREAMS

LITTLE NIGHTMARES, LITTLE DREAMS

RACHEL SIMON

Houghton Mifflin/Seymour Lawrence

BOSTON 1990

For information about permission to reproduce selections from
this book, write to Permissions, Houghton Mifflin Company,
2 Park Street, Boston, Massachusetts 02108.

Library of Congress Cataloging-in-Publication Data

Simon, Rachel, date.
Little nightmares, little dreams / Rachel Simon.
p.   cm.
ISBN 0-89919-952-6
I. Title.
PS3569.I4845L5   1990   90-34798
813'.54 — dc20   CIP

Printed in the United States of America

BP 10 9 8 7 6 5 4 3 2 1

Some of the stories in this collection have appeared elsewhere,
in slightly different form: "Little Nightmares, Little Dreams" in
Story, "Breath of This Night" in *Missouri Review Online* and
College Magazine, "Skirts" in *Quarterly West*, "Paint" in *The
North American Review*, "Grandma Death" in *North Dakota Review*,
"Magnet Hill" in *The Antietam Review*, and "Afterglow"
in *Witness*.

For HAL, *who keeps me dreaming*

Acknowledgments

This book was supported jointly by grants from the Pennsylvania Council on the Arts and the Ludwig Vogelstein Foundation. I am very grateful for their timely and generous assistance.

I would also like to thank the following institutions and individuals for their guidance, encouragement, and friendship: the Virginia Center for the Creative Arts; the students and faculty of the University of Pennsylvania and Sarah Lawrence College, especially Diana Cavallo, Romulus Linney, Chuck Wachtel, and Linsey Abrams; Philomena Baylor, Margaret Broucek, Mitchell A. Cohn, Patricia Hamill, Marshall Hill, Mark Kramer, Deborah Lincoln Lear, Ellen Michaelson, Dani Shapiro, and Woody; my agent, Irene Skolnick, my publisher, Seymour Lawrence, and his associate Camille Hykes, and, most importantly, my editor, Fran Kiernan.

It was only with you that I did it.

Contents

LITTLE NIGHTMARES, LITTLE DREAMS / 1

BREATH OF THIS NIGHT / 15

SKIRTS / 21

THE GREATEST MYSTERY OF THEM ALL / 37

TRAINS / 53

TWINS / 59

HEARTS / 79

PAINT / 85

THE LONG SADNESS OF NO / 107

GRANDMA DEATH / 113

MAGNET HILL / 125

LAUNCHING THE ECHO / 139

THE SECRET LIVES OF MY TOYS / 147

SHEETS / 155

AFTERGLOW / 171

SINCE NANNA CAME TO STAY / 191

LITTLE
NIGHTMARES,
LITTLE DREAMS

AND NOW, he wants us to share our dreams. Not just talk about them in the morning over coffee, like we usually do. He means we should dream them together, at the same time. Try doing it this very afternoon.

I say to him, "Fabian, isn't it enough we've been married fifty-three years, that we've known no one in a biblical way but each other, and we've always made a point of having a real conversation every night in bed? That sounds about as close as any two people can get. This doctor you've been seeing — did he put something funny into one of those pills?"

"No," Fabian says, and he lowers his teacup to the saucer. He's used saucers since the day we were married. I like how he respects the furniture, even now that he's retired, sitting around eating cream cheese sandwiches and listening to talk shows on the radio. He never leaves a ring on the wood. Not even after he's bought a can of soda on the way back from the doctor, and when he makes it up the front steps all he can do is fall into the nearest chair. Even then, he remembers to use a coaster.

He says, "Elsie, maybe there are ways to get even closer. Wouldn't that be something — dreaming together?"

"Yeah, it'd be something."

"And I think I know how we can manage it. I've been doing some reading. Seems like it might just be a matter of physical position and will." I look at him, smile, and shake my head. "Come on, Elsie. It'll be easy. It'll be worth it."

This is what he said about all his get-closer ideas, and he's been pushing them since the night he carried me over the threshold. First it was doing the marital act with the lights on. This was not too hard for me, as I was young and curious about the curves and angles of the human body which I'd never been privileged to see before. Then, it was using the commode with the door open. I resisted this till I started shuffling diapers like stacks of soiled playing cards. After that, who can be modest? It's no longer a secret what happens at the far end of our intestines. And, of course, those talks at night. His idea. And a good one too, I came to see. Those talks kept us linked all through the problems of loud music and sibling wars and dreary wedding ceremonies and two-home grandchildren.

I used to wonder why it mattered so much to him to be close. This was not what people I knew expected out of marriage. He couldn't have gotten the idea from the relatives who raised him. They were private people. They were good people — if a few too many in number. Once we took a vacation and drove by all his old homes; our route looked like we'd dropped a handful of lentils on the map of the United States, and they'd scattered to every corner.

His only buddies — besides me, that is — have been my girlfriends' husbands. Married couples would come to our house and split apart the moment they stepped inside, the wives drawing me away to the kitchen so we could talk about our marriages and children, the husbands urging Fabian to come out front and see the new car, or play a few rounds of gin rummy. Now, the few friends who visit come alone; they've all become widows. Fabian, for the last few years, took classes at the community center downtown. Legends of Imaginary Animals, Extraterrestrial Influence in Human History. I'd ask him, "Did you meet anyone?" He'd shrug, "Yes, but they're too busy. Everyone's too busy." Recently he stopped going, saying the doctor visits take enough out of him as it is. Now all he does is sit in the house or backyard, reading and listening to the radio. With such a life, I'd be lonely. But he says he doesn't need anyone except me.

The closeness Fabian and I have had, it's satisfied us both. Till the last few months, that is. Suddenly, get-close ideas are all he thinks about. Why, just a few weeks ago he set up two checkerboards, one in my sewing room upstairs, the other in his toolshed out back. My set had the red pieces, his the black. He said, "You move one man every other night, I go on the nights in between." "How will I know where your men are?" I asked. "Marriage ESP," he said.

Now, sitting beside me in the kitchen, he says, "So I found this dream book at that flea market where I got those embroidered handkerchiefs you like so much. And this book, it says there are ways to dream together."

"You know, you've also read books that said the sun was going to blink off at six A.M. Christmas Day three years ago. And then there was that whole Inca power series you thought was so good."

"I know, I know. But those books, they didn't give me any ideas on how *we* can make our lives better. They were just interesting to think about."

"They were." This I had to admit.

Fabian says, "Let me show you the book. Then you can decide." He gets up and shuffles across the linoleum to the living room. The sun's coming through the window, lighting up his hair like a crown.

Fabian's still the most handsome man I've ever seen. Though to be truthful, since I got to be able to tell time by the different ways my limbs creak during the day, I have been noticing younger men. There's one that lives across the street, divorced, women in and out of there every few days like he keeps trying them on but can't find the one that suits him. He's good-looking, this man; I almost want to put on rouge when I take out the garbage.

Still, other men, though I think about them, they're nothing to me. It's been so long since Fabian and I walked up the aisle. Then and now, we keep each other from falling. That's what those talks before bed are about. Holding out our arms as we stumble through life together, working each other loose if one of us gets stuck in some bad situation.

He comes back into the kitchen, lays the book on the table. It's dusty, smells like a basement, has mold crawling across the cover. *The Greatest Intimacy.* I have to put on my glasses; the words are hard to read, all squiggly like dripping batter. Like those posters Peggy used to pin to her wall back when she kept skipping school and staying in her room all day, smoking what kids did then, we later found out.

"Looks like one of those Leary treatises," I say.

"Don't knock it, Elsie," he says. "Not everyone back then was a — what did James used to call them?"

"Airhead."

"Yeah. Give it a chance, don't fight this like you did some of my other ideas."

The book crackles as I open it. Fabian lowers himself slowly into the chair. "I picked this up because of that talk we had a few nights ago, remember? That talk where you said — how'd you put it? — that we could lay the maze of our minds on top of each other and they'd lock together just about perfectly."

He was right, I'd said that. Me and my mouth. I say

6

things that sound grand, and I don't mean them fully. See, he'd been talking about entering us in this Couple of the Year contest the local park's planning to hold in a few weeks. Couples will sit under a tent and get asked questions to see how well they know each other. Like some game on TV, I'm told, though we don't watch TV. Anyway, I said then that we were a shoo-in if we entered. Being married so long, we don't even need to talk, when it comes to things like what's for dinner and what our bodies are feeling and what mood we're in. The kinds of questions I expect they'd ask in that contest. Skin questions, as Peggy called them when she was on her anti-superficiality kick. Nothing that shows you really *know* someone, know the parts of him he can't put into words himself. Maybe even know something before he does.

Truth is, though I admire Fabian's get-close ideas, I'm of the opinion — and I do tell him this from time to time, but he likes to forget — that you have to have some private place inside you. Not for secrets, necessarily, though that's nice too. But for a feeling of yourself and what it means to be alone, on two legs instead of four. Because I'm no fool, I know it's all good now, but the time will come when one of us will be gone. Then where will the survivor be, if our I's have always been we's? I'll tell you, this is my little nightmare.

But I said what I said, and in marriage the words you speak to your mate are never forgotten. "So you really want to do this. But I still don't even know if we're playing the same game of checkers."

"We'll look at each other's boards tomorrow, OK? And as for this dreaming stuff — it'll be fun. At the very least, we'll have a nice afternoon together in bed. And it's been a while since we've taken naps together, hasn't it?"

I think for a second. "Only about forty-five years."

"So we're long overdue."

"Well, what makes it happen? Some weird contraption? Hypnosis?"

"Says here" — and he flips through the book — "that all you have to do is lie on your backs with the arms that meet in the middle hooked together and the arms on the sides propped up on pillows. Says doing it in daylight is good too, because the sleep levels don't drop as low, so it's more likely you can dream."

"Sounds a little too easy."

"Humor me."

"First, tell me this: Do you make up a dream together? Or does one of you start and then the other joins in?"

"It didn't go into that," he says, pushing his bifocals up on his nose and turning to the dog-eared pages. Then he looks at me. "Does it matter?"

Well, actually it might. For the past few weeks, Fabian's felt tired all day long. He keeps calling the doctor, who tells him to come by for more tests. They've tried five different kinds of medicine so far. I offer to go with him, but he's got too much pride to let me come along, and I don't push the issue. So, when he leaves, I lie on the beach chair on the front porch and wait for him to return. And this is why dreaming together might matter: once, while I was on that chair, I took a little nap, and dreamt about the man across the street. I'm almost embarrassed to admit it — in the dream the man took me into his house and, well, I actually felt a little guilty when I woke up. But now, sitting here across the table from Fabian, thinking about that dream, I realize: once the clothes came off, I was no longer with the man across the street; I was with my husband. "No, it doesn't matter," I say.

I peer at him, with his white hair and white eyebrows, his brown eyes the color of coffee. Except for this dream with the man across the street, I don't do anything without Fabian at my side in my dreams. He's like the smell of my own body, the way my hair feels on my neck — something I don't think about, he's so much a part of me. And it's nice, because when my dreams fade into waking, he's next to me still.

Sometimes I forget what Fabian looks like. I forget I'm there too; I can just feel us together. This is the opposite of how it was when we first met, my eyes following his lips as he spoke to me, following the skimming of his fingers over my porch railing as we stood in the brisk winter chill. I watched him so closely, I swear I could see his cells reproduce. When I turned away, it was only because my parents were calling me inside.

In marriage, for years, this was how it went too. With each other but separate. Especially in our bed: very *me* and *he*. Air all around us, between us. Two bodies touching self-consciously, even when in rhythm hearing our own inner beat.

Then — when did it happen? And how? The difference between me and Fabian just seemed to disappear. This even when we had to lock the door to keep the kids out, or when Barbara ran away to Montana and we were so worried. This even through my fifties, when my hormones surfed out of me on waves of sweat, and I dried up inside my private parts. And I can remember when our last grandchild was born. We got off the phone and stretched out on the sofa. Even there, we fell into step, didn't hear anything but our own breathing, mixing with the sighing of the furnace. And this is how it is now, even when all we do is lie back and hold each other.

"Come on," he says, rising to his feet and tugging on the sleeve of my housedress.

"You wanted to try marijuana too, after we read about

it in *Life* magazine," I tell him. "Look where we'd be now if we'd done that."

He shrugs. "As bad off as Louise, but as good as Peggy. Who can say what will happen?" He lowers his head and coughs. "Please. Do this for me."

I tell him, "All right. OK. I'll try it this once."

We go upstairs. I have to walk beside him on the steps so I can hold his elbow for support. I move slowly because lately he's had to.

In our bedroom he lowers the shade. The afternoon sun lights it up from behind, and the shadows of branches and leaves lie across it like lace.

I stand by the bed. He comes toward me. I raise my arms, and he works my dress over my hips, belly, breasts, head. Then he peels off my underthings. I am doing this to him too, unbuttoning, unbelting.

We lie down. There is no blanket, just sheets, and we do not get under them. We breathe, the window shade taps against the sill. What does my body look like? My friends complain about theirs, about how fat or thin or weak they are, about how their imperfect bodies made them avoid intimacy when their husbands were alive. Me, somehow I always forget to notice my body when I'm with Fabian. And he's with me all the time; I am never naked alone.

Always we roll to face each other. But this time we don't. Instead we each take one of the extra pillows at the top of the bed and fit it beneath our outside elbows.

"And now what do we do?" I ask.

"We lock arms," he says.

He lifts his left arm and hooks it into my right.

"What do you want to dream about?" I ask him.

"I don't know. I just want to see what happens."

We lie there, looking at the ceiling. A few cars buzz by outside. A little girl down the street calls for her friend.

Then I start giggling, and in a moment Fabian joins in. There we are in bed, in this crazy position, laughing. "I feel too silly to do this," I say.

"So do I," he says. "Wouldn't you just die if the kids could see us?"

This makes me laugh more. I go on like this for a while, the laughter rolling out of me, the bed trembling. I go on until I realize Fabian is no longer laughing with me, and then it occurs to me that I feel more nervous than silly. I am panting as I laugh, the way a child does when he's lying.

I close my eyes. Fabian is breathing deeply already. He twitches, that teetering-on-the-edge-of-sleep twitch. I follow his breath like it is a broom sweeping my path clear. Time passes, I think I will never get there, I jolt awake, I sink back down.

And then finally I fall asleep.

The dream opens to me slowly. We are sitting on the sofa in our living room. At first this dream feels no different from any other; how can I tell if Fabian is having it too? "Are you with me?" I ask him. "I think so," he says, but a look flashes across his face and then he adds, "Where are we?" "We're at home," I say, "See? There's the lamp Louise made in school and the family photograph we got for our fortieth anniversary and that fern you bought last week." "Yes," he says, "I see."

Someone knocks on the front door. Fabian rises to answer and, since our arms are locked together, even in this dream, I must rise with him. Side by side we make our way across the room.

When we open the door, the porch is empty. But then Fabian says, "Is that a man or a woman?" as he peers into the darkness.

I am not sure if I should tell him I don't see anyone. I

can feel him getting scared. "What are you doing, just standing there?" he asks the invisible — to me — stranger. "What do you want from me?"

I turn to Fabian. His eyes are wide, and he is sweating. "Is this your dream?" I ask him. "Or is it mine?"

"It's not my dream," he says, still staring ahead. "It's my nightmare."

My back tingles and I look away from him, down at my legs. They're thick and netted with varicose veins. My eyes sweep up my body and I see myself now, as if I'm naked for the first time in my life. The dimples on my stomach, the wrinkles that fan down my breasts, my navel gaping like an open mouth. So this is how I look.

I want to tell him this, and I raise my head to speak directly to him. But it is in that moment that I wake up.

He is still beside me, breathing deeply. I look at his profile. I know every pore on that face.

Lying there, watching him, this is what I feel: his nightmare was telling me something. Though maybe it was *my* nightmare, and all it was doing was making clear a fact I've suspected for the past few weeks but haven't wanted to face. And maybe I haven't faced it because he hasn't yet, either.

I unlock my arm from his and sit up. I could wake him to ask what he dreamt, see if it overlapped in any way with what I dreamt. I want to; but I can't bring myself to do that. Not right now.

I roll off the bed and throw on my dress. In the dying sunlight I see his body, white and covered with hair, his love handles and the smiles under his knees. I leave the bedroom and close the door.

Light no longer shines into the hallway, so it must be near dusk. I walk downstairs. I'm not sure why I don't go to my sewing room, where his shirts sit in my basket, waiting for buttons. I have let them pile up for months; now I wonder if I can finish them in time.

I go through the living room and the kitchen, out the back door. The sky is deep blue, receding into black at the tree line. I pad across the grass, noticing his sandals, a book he was reading, a glass half empty. When I reach the tool-shed, I hear crickets, rising around me like hymns.

It is dark inside the shed. I have to wave my arms in the air as I creep forward until one hand brushes against the hanging light bulb. I click it on.

Everything — floor, tools, worktable — is covered with sawdust, as it was the last time I was in here. When was that? At least a few years. But there is regular dust now too, thick on everything, even the air. Well, almost everything. Not the checkerboard.

I walk over and look down. A few of his checkers sit along the side of the table. I guess he thought I jumped them. I close my eyes and try to envision my whole board. That man here, that one there, those three kings. . . . And when the picture is sharp, I open my eyes and lay it on top of the board in front of me. He was right, we can play the same game without even looking. We do have marriage ESP.

On the chair in front of the board is one of his shirts, a red flannel shirt that he wore all last winter. It has no dust on it. I pick it up and hold it to my face. It smells like a shirt; no, like *his* shirt. He does have a smell, I just never notice it; I forget and think it is me.

I lift my dress up over my head and drop it on the chair. Then I fit myself into his shirt. It is large. I don't button it; I wrap it around me, like his arms.

It is dark when I make my way across the yard, back into the house, and upstairs. I feel my way along the wall. The house is so quiet when I think of him gone.

In our room I raise the shade, and moonlight beams in. He looks like he's covered with snow. As I sit on the bed, he groans and turns his head toward me.

13

"You're up?" he says.

"Not for long," I say. "What did you dream?"

"Oh," he says, rubbing his eyes, rolling over to face the ceiling. "I couldn't figure out where I was." He pauses for a moment. "You were with me. I asked you where we were, and you said we were at home. But it didn't look like home to me. It looked like a combination of the houses I grew up in. Familiar and strange at the same time.

"And then there was a knock on the door. I had to tug on your hand to get you up to answer it. I opened the door, and there was — someone or something. Not really a person. I asked who it was, and it wouldn't answer, it just stood there, staring. I wanted to lock it out, but when I turned to ask you to help me close the door, you were looking down, away from me. That thing — I was looking at it again — wanted me to step onto the porch. I didn't want to, but I couldn't walk away. All I could do was stand there like I was frozen. And then I realized that you weren't holding my hand anymore; you were gone. It was just me and it. And we stared at each other so long . . ."

My skin grows cold beneath his shirt; I grab it tighter around me. "Fabian," I say, "that was the same dream I had."

"I knew we could do it," he says, but he doesn't sound happy. He takes hold of my hand. "It scared me, Elsie. It made me feel like something terrible's going to happen. Did you feel that? Did you feel that in your dream?"

I want to reply that it won't be terrible, but I know it will. And I cannot be dishonest; after all, we have marriage ESP. I lie down on the bed and stroke his chest. His hair tickles my palm. I have not been aware of this, of him and me, for so long now. "Fabian," I whisper, telling myself to remember how his hair feels beneath my hand, how his body feels next to mine, "I'm sure we'll be all right."

BREATH
OF THIS NIGHT

I HAVE THREE DAUGHTERS, young, pink, and brimming with questions. People tell me I am too young to have so many children. After college — bing! bing! bing! They came as if my life was a book in the wind, flipping madly to the chapter where the spine was made to bend. I love my little girls, my bevy of beauties. At night I gather them around me in their matching nightgowns of flannel rosebushes. I put the light on low, so my room looks golden and streaked with shadows, like the field behind our house at the end of the day.

They climb all around the bed and sprawl across my legs, propping up their heads. "Tell us about when you were a little girl, Mommy."

And I ask, "What do you want to know?" There is so much to tell. Games, friends, schools, clothes. But always they pick the same thing:

"Tell us about rock 'n' roll."

These children. These babies suckling the curdled milk of Madonna. What do they know of rock 'n' roll? Only that at one time it was more adventurous, more passionate. A time when old men, men now their father's age, stood outside the world and made it come to them. A time when their mother was a child, sitting in the backyard with her brother's transistor, hearing for the first time the deejays and melodies and harmonies of AM radio. "Radio!" "How'd they show videos?" "Is AM anything like B.C.?"

So they lie there and I tell them about the garage band on the corner, spraying my street every Sunday with guitar solos and Farfisa organ; the light show at the school dance, where transparencies netted with India ink were slapped wet and wriggling onto an overhead projector. I tell them about my first forty-five. I tell them about my first concert. "The Yardbirds," I say, gushing. "Who's that?" my girls ask. I smile and tell them, "That's where the guitarist in The Firm came from."

One night I tell them about when my brother took me to Woodstock, and all the people there, and how the bathroom lines were too long. "We couldn't find a space as big as this bed to sit on." I tell them to imagine an ocean full of people instead of water. "Oooh," says Marjorie, the middle one, the one who believes in magic. Her round eyes echo the shape of her mouth. Liza, the youngest, asks, "Does that mean that when it rained, people fell from the skies?"

Tonight they ask me again. "Rock 'n' roll," they say. And I wonder what to tell them. Nothing after Woodstock; hairs began sprouting in new places on my body after Woodstock. I am not ready for them to meet up with puberty.

So I tell them this story. It's a little story, lost for many years in my nightly rush of memories. I'm not even sure if I've ever mentioned it to my husband. I was in second grade. "Your age, Claudia," I say to the oldest. Her face sits buried behind glasses, and she does not smile often. But for this, she grins.

"My neighbors, Emily and Wanda," I say, "were very rich, and their daddy worked in New York. One night he took them to see — the Rolling Stones."

18

They squeal, even Claudia, and roll all over the bed. The Rolling Stones, those trilobites of the Golden Age, those Angry Old Men, those Methuselahs whose wrinkles these young eyes so effortlessly iron out.

"And the next day, Emily came over and brought me the Rolling Stones' breath."

"How do you carry breath?" Claudia asks. Liza cups her hands, the tiniest in the room, and blows into them.

I say, "They trapped it in a bottle. A little vitamin jar. Their father typed up a label that said, 'Rolling Stones' Breath,' and the date."

"Wow," Liza says.

"That's better than having a genie," Marjorie says.

"No it's not," Claudia says. "I bet all their daddy did was open up a bottle in the theater and then close it."

Marjorie protests. "But it's still got the Rolling Stones' breath in it."

"Breath is just air. That's what my teacher says."

"But Rolling Stone breath is special breath," Liza says.

"All breath's the same."

The two younger girls begin to wilt. "No," I say. "Everyone's breath is special because it only comes once, and then it's gone. It's like taking a picture, except you can't see what it looks like." Liza sucks her thumb with her eyes closed; Marjorie makes half-hearted hand shadows on the wall. I lean forward and touch their knees. "You know," I say, "I wish I could keep all your breath, from the day you were born."

"You do?" Liza and Marjorie say, peering up at me, thumbs and shadows forgotten. I glance at Claudia. For a moment her eyebrows knit together as if she is working on a difficult arithmetic problem. But only for a moment.

Because then I say, "I know. Let's save some tonight." And I grab their hands and we make a chain and jump off the bed and run downstairs, the four of us, even Claudia, giggling like sisters. In the kitchen I rummage around until I find four jars. Liza breathes in one. Immediately I screw on the lid and label it. Then Marjorie goes. Then me. Claudia almost refuses. "No," she says, watching us. I begin to label hers "Empty," and Liza and Marjorie wail and groan. Claudia stares at her jar, then pushes me away and exhales into it as if she is blowing up the biggest balloon in the world.

Later, I line the four jars along my headboard. Someday, when I am old, and my husband is dead, and my children have children who ask about rock 'n' roll, I will open those jars. I'll turn the lids slowly, and sniff the contents like fine wines. I'll put my face into each jar, as deep as the opening will allow, and breathe in my children's breath. And I will remember this night. Suspended for long, then lost in an instant. So much, I'll think then, like a flower under glass, crumbling into dust when its petals touch the air.

SKIRTS

HE'S NO DIFFERENT. That's what I thought at first. He's
a townie from the streets like the rest of them. They come
by, I do it with them, give them blow jobs, whatever. Him
too, but he's not like them. They're easy. He's not. He asks
why I do it. I don't have to tell anyone why.

What do I do it for? Can't say. The college shrink has
some ideas. R.A. walked by in September just as three town-
ies were leaving my room. I was standing in the doorway,
wearing a button-down shirt, nothing else. Standard op-
erating procedure. She looks at me, peeks into my room,
recoils. "You're crazy, girl," she says. She tells on me.
There's a big uproar, they say I have to get therapy or they'll
tell my mother. I land in the shrink's office the next day.

I have to change where I do it, so the R.A. won't know.
I get word out to the guys; I lived in town last summer, I
know how to reach them. I tell them, Meet me at the end
of campus, by the brook behind Physical Plant, four o'clock
every day. It's still light then, and all the janitors are gone.
I bring a blanket, a radio. Some Fig Newtons and M&M's.
Have my jeans off before they arrive.

They come in groups, mostly. Two, three. They've got
long hair and their backs are greasy. What do you expect

when all they do is panhandle from the tourists in town and sleep in the Revolutionary War park at night? Sometimes their pubic hair's tangled. Sometimes they watch before it's their turn.

I don't know their names. A few tried to tell me, but I told them, Who cares, and they shut up. To myself I think of them like famous writers. Byron, Lawrence, Wilde.

This new guy, he wasn't around last summer. I call him Lewis. For Carroll. He comes alone. I mean, he comes every day, waits behind a tree until he's sure no one else's showing up. Then he pops out like he just got there.

He's older than the others. Got white streaks in his hair, wears a suit with holes all through it. First time he showed up, he says, "You got a skirt? I prefer to do it with skirts." "No," I say, "I don't wear clothes like that, only men's jeans, jockey shorts." He reaches into his pants pocket, grabs hold of a white scarf, pulls and pulls and pulls. When it's all out, it's the biggest scarf I've ever seen. "Stand up," he says. He gives me a corner to hold, then walks around me seven times — I count them — until he's wrapped me almost as tight as a mummy from my waist to my knees. Fastens it with a safety pin he takes from behind his ear. "Now stand in the brook," he says. I walk in there, almost slip on the wet rocks. He doesn't take off his pants. He knows what he's doing. He barely even wrinkles the skirt.

His skin smells stale and wooden, like a rotting house on a lake. The hair on his head's stiff as mannequin hair.

He takes a long time. After, he asks about my orgasm. Nobody ever asks that. It's a myth, I tell him, that girls have them. For us, that's not what it's about.

"Then what's it about?" he says.

"None of your business," I say. "Some girls scratch their arms till they bleed. I do this."

Every time he shows up, he stays longer. I take it for

24 .

granted I'll get to the dining hall too late for dinner. So I lie around on the blanket when he's done, eating my Fig Newtons. The sun's down by then, but there's some light from the path in front of Physical Plant. Lewis likes to stay with me. I listen to the radio, watch the skirt ripple in the breeze. He smokes a joint.

We don't say much. That's how I like it.

My shrink thinks she's sewed me up, that because of her, no man gets inside me. She crosses her legs under her full skirts, crosses her arms against her silk blouses. Her hair's as meticulously styled as a model's. Just like my mother's. That's why I wear a fedora, sometimes — to cover my hair. The shrink and my mother, they must spend two hours every day getting ready for the world. They must practice their smiles in the mirror when they're done, making sure the corners curl up to just the right height.

"Summer's ending too quickly for me this year," she says when I sit down. "Would you like some tea?" She lifts a white porcelain teapot and holds the spout above the lip of a matching cup.

No.

Her hand freezes, then she lowers the pot without pouring. "So," she says, leaning back, "have things improved since your last visit?"

There's nothing to improve, I say. I'm fine.

"You look good. Like you're getting more sleep."

It's still five hours most nights, four.

Her eyes get wide. "That's little more than a nap. Do you sleep straight through?"

No. Never.

"What happens when you wake up?"

I lie there. Concentrate on the books I'm reading, keeping my eyes closed.

"You don't open your eyes?"

No.

"Why? Some sort of test?"

I don't need to test myself.

"Have you ever slept more than you sleep now?"

Yeah. Weekends when I stayed with my mother. She used to say girls needed beauty rest. She'd put me to bed at nine, wouldn't let me get up till seven or eight. Checked on me during the night to make sure I was still asleep.

"How did you know that, if you were asleep?"

I could feel her. I'd be half-awake and I could feel her in the doorway, watching me.

"Did that scare you?"

I don't get scared. I'd just roll over and sleep some more.

She looks at me like I'm a war refugee. She pulls out a pad and asks about my father (disappeared before I ever knew him), my uncles (send stock reports, never visit), my mother's father (came by once, didn't meet him). She asks if my mother had boyfriends. Yeah, after she sent me to school. Rich guys who worked in big companies. The maid told me about them. They took my mother to company functions, dropped her off before eleven o'clock. She'd walk in sober as a stone, her dress clear of wrinkles, her hair perfect in its mold. She'd ask the maid to leave the lights on all night. She'd go to bed.

"What did you think of her dates?" the shrink asks.

Nothing. Never met them. I imagine they were all frustrated, couldn't get anywhere with her.

She scribbles. She asks more about men. She goes on and on, like if she lists enough, she'll hit on the one who did me wrong. Like she's going to win the lottery by buying every ticket.

It doesn't get her anywhere. Because, truth is, no man made me do this. *I* made me do this. Not for fun. Just for.

Why do people chop off their arms? Why do people burn down their houses with their children inside?

The days begin to get cold. I cut off all my hair. I've been making it shorter and shorter since last school year, and now I go at it until I can rest the sides of the scissors on my head as I clip. The cactus look.

Lewis, when he's done one day, walks me over to the blanket, takes off his jacket, drapes it on me. I wiggle around beneath it so none of the holes leads directly to my skin. I hate being cold.

He sits next to me, lights a joint, offers it to me. I tell him I don't do drugs. He laughs a little — first time I ever heard him laugh — coughs, spits, drags. Sounds sick, like he's got cancer.

When he's down to the roach, he says to me, "What're you doing here?"

"Lying down. Watching the tops of the trees, the stars."

"No," he says. "I mean in this school. This girls' school."

"I've always been in girls' schools. My mother sticks me in them. She wishes she'd gone to them. She thinks they're safe."

"But in school, any school. You don't seem to belong."

"You don't think I'm smart?"

"I couldn't know. You don't say much."

I listen to the water trickle between the rocks. Far away someone turns up a stereo. "I like it here," I say. "It's a nice place to live. I can do what I want. I get to read."

He lies back, puts his hands behind his head for a pillow. "I used to read," he says. "But reading keeps you alone too much."

"I like being alone."

"You could've surprised me."

"This is like being alone."

27

He looks my way, waits a second. Then blows out a laugh like a bullet from a gun.

The shrink is dipping a tea bag in a cup of water when I come in. I'm fifteen minutes late. She doesn't say anything about the time. She says, "I got some hot chocolate for you."

I don't want any, I say, though my mouth tingles when I think of the chocolate sliding down my throat, thick and warm as semen. I sit and look at the collection of ceramic lions on the shelf behind her head. The males stand with their chests thrust out, their manes wild; the females lie cute and hairless, huddling around the cubs.

That's such sentimental crap, I say. Idealized. Sometimes lions eat their young, did you know that? If they're inexperienced and don't know what they're doing? They think the cubs will attract predators to the den. So they eat them.

"Do you think your mother ever felt that way?"

My mother? What way.

"Threatened or confused enough to try to destroy you."

My mother doesn't feel anything.

"Did you ever see her cry?"

She doesn't cry. She'll tell you that. She takes showers.

"Do you cry?"

Not now. When I was a kid I did. She used to brush my hair out every day. She'd rip through the knots. I'd cry. I'd tell her to stop but she wouldn't till the brush made it from my scalp to my waist in one clean stroke.

"You had hair that long?"

Longer, even. She made me set it so the ends curled. So it looked perfect, and people would see it and know we were a respectable family. First time I ever got it cut was last May. Chopped it off myself. Used the gardener's clippers. She wouldn't let me stay home last summer because of it.

"It must have been very painful when she told you that."

No. Years ago it might have. But not now. I know what I'm doing now.

"If you weren't hurt, what did you feel?"

Cold.

"In May?"

Yeah. Even thinking about her coming to visit me here again. Looking at my hair, what I'm wearing. The thought makes me cold.

North wind blows in, leaves scuttle around the banks of the brook. Some days I wear a tie. Some days I draw a mustache over my lip with an eyeliner, sideburns below my ears. I wear them to class, touch them up before I leave for the brook with my blanket. That's when I put on after-shave lotion, sometimes.

Lewis's jacket is not long enough to cover my legs. And the skirt's too thin to do any good. One day, I sit up, go to put on my pants. "No," he says. "Wear mine." He stands up, unzips, pulls them off. I ease them on beneath the skirt. They're wool. When the wind hits them, it feels like waves of insects scrambling up my legs.

Lewis sits in his shirt and underwear. "You may wonder how I can sit in the cold," he says, sucking on a joint. He points to his head. "It's control, self-control. Knowing I direct my own show, that I can take care of myself. I'd be crazy by now if I didn't have it."

"You don't direct this show," I say.

He scratches his chin, looks at the skirt, then up at my face. "No," he says, "I don't suppose I do."

I grab a Fig Newton, stick the whole thing in my mouth, chew while I talk. "What'd you read?" I say.

"What?"

"What'd you read, when you read?"

"Just about anything. I taught English." He waves his

29

hand. "That way, a few towns over. It was a good life. I'd go back if I could."

I try to imagine him teaching me, in his dirty shirt and underwear. I bet he did it with his students, he's the type. For a second I wonder if I'd have slipped him a note after class, asking him to meet me in the janitor's closet at lunch like I did with Mr. Wallace. Or if I'd have just stopped by his office after school one day, snapped off the light, stripped off my clothes. Like what happened with Mr. Reed that one time.

I wore skirts in high school. Had to. My mother'd thrown all my other clothes in the garbage, everything that wasn't proper and feminine. Checked my closet when she came to visit once, turned around and faced me like I'd betrayed her. Yanked everything off the hangers, the floor. Carried it outside in a big bundle, pitched it into the dumpster. Right in front of the other students. After that, she had copies of her own skirts made. That's what I got for my birthdays, then.

I was always cold, especially outside. The winter air would snake between my legs, tickle my crotch. I wanted to bind my thighs together to keep myself warm. She wouldn't even let me wear knee socks or pantyhose. Only stockings, the kind she wore, with lace at the top. She'd make surprise visits to check up on me.

Lewis would have liked me then. Dressed so nice, looking so fine. Wearing all the right clothes. Skirts.

"Who're your friends?" the shrink says.

I don't much like people, I say.

"But you're a literature student. Literature's about people."

Oh, yeah. But they're not real people. They're better than real. You can close the book when you want.

"Those men — you couldn't make them leave when you wanted."

Sure I could. I'm in control with them. I'm in control with everything here. My work. Myself.

"But, honey, for any woman, what you did with those men was a way of giving up all your control."

Maybe for other girls. Not for me.

"But don't you see, that they could have done anything to you?"

No they couldn't have. They did what I told them.

"Did *you* always do what you were told?"

When I was at my mother's house. Sure.

"Always?"

Once I didn't. It was after dinner. I was getting ready for bed, and she ran upstairs and told me to leave.

"Leave for good?"

Leave. Take a walk. There was a man coming up the driveway. She told me she didn't want him to see me.

"And you didn't leave?"

No, I did, I left. Threw on a robe. She ran me down the back stairs and shut me outside.

"And then?"

And then I walked around. It was January — no ice, but all I had on was my nightgown and the robe and the wind was blowing like mad. I hid and watched him go inside, then checked out his car. The plates were a name instead of numbers, that's how I realized it was her father. The engine was still warm. I sat on the hood till it cooled.

Then I went to the kitchen door, tried to sneak in. Only she'd locked it. I walked around to find a window to climb through. That's when I saw him standing in the living room. His arms were going wild, looked like he was yelling at her.

"What was she doing?"

Kind of cringing. Kneading the seat of the chair with her hands. Not saying anything. Her face was red.

"And what did you do?"

Tried to figure out what was happening. Kept shaking the cold out of my hands. Finally it got the better of me. I ran around the house. All the doors were locked. Felt like my toes were breaking away from my body. We have this trellis with vines on it. I ran to that and climbed it. I didn't think I'd be able to hold on, my fingers were just frozen. And the wind was so cold, it felt like it was slapping me. Oh, just thinking about it. . . . But I got in. I climbed through my bedroom window.

"Did she find out you disobeyed?"

She went to her room right after he left. Turned on her shower. I waited a few minutes, then tiptoed downstairs, to see what would've happened if I hadn't climbed in. And you know what? The doors were still locked. She'd forgotten me. I would've frozen to death. Can you believe that? Can you fucking believe that? And she didn't even mention it the next morning. She didn't even mention it ever.

"Are you OK? Would you like a tissue?"

No. I'm fine.

"You sure?"

I'm fine.

"Did this happen before or after you started sleeping with men?"

What?

"How soon after this did you become sexually active?"

She sent me away to school after this. To another girls' school, but away.

"The men — when did that start?"

Men? I don't know.

"When you went away to school?"

Couldn't have been before that. Couldn't breathe if she didn't want me to.

"So it started after you left. Do you have any idea why?"

What?

"Can you think of why you started to do what you did?"

. . . I don't have to answer you, you know. I can just get up and leave.

"But those men — they didn't help you with anything."

They don't need to help me. I don't need help. I can do whatever I want.

"Can? You're not still doing it, are you?"

Whatever I do, it's my business.

"Oh, honey —"

It's my business. It's *my* business. I have to go now. I have a test. I have to go.

I skip my next appointment. The shrink calls me at my dorm and asks what's wrong.

I don't want to come anymore, I tell her.

"Why?"

I don't have anything to say.

"But there's so much to discuss."

There's nothing to discuss. Leave me alone.

"I know you don't want to come back, but trust me — you're in trouble."

I'm fine.

"Will you just consider coming in for one more session?"

I have too much work.

"Then remember I'll be here to help you, if you need someone. I'm concerned about you."

Sure, I'll remember. When I need someone, that's when I'll call.

★

33

The first frost makes our bed stiff and hard. I wear my jeans, my shirt, his wool pants, his tattered jacket. I unpin the skirt and wrap it around my head for a hat.

"You're not going to leave it there, are you?" Lewis says.

"Yeah. My head's cold."

He unbuttons his shirt, holds it out to me. "Pin this on, then," he says.

His nipples come out like the stars at night. Goose bumps coat his chest, making it look textured, perforated. He's got no hair on his body, except of course the part still covered by his briefs.

I say, "I can't do this, take your shirt."

He leans over me, lowers the shirt onto my pelvis. "Lift up," he says. I raise myself just a little, just enough for him to slip the shirt behind me. He ties a knot by my hip with the sleeves.

"You're going to freeze to death," I say.

"Then hold me close," he says.

I don't want to. My hands are cold. I'm afraid to touch him, in that way. He lies beside me, turns me on my side, presses his chest to me. I can barely feel him through the clothes. I put my arm out, drape it around his back. Slowly, I rest my fingers on his opposite shoulder blade. His goose bumps feel as large as blisters.

"You must be freezing," I say.

"No," he says.

I don't want to touch him. I try to push myself back, away from him. "Don't do that," he says. I stop. I take my hand off his shoulder and swing my arm in front of me. It stretches straight down, between us, toward his pants. He wriggles nearer. He pushes up against my arm.

I know what I want. I start to slide my hand inside his briefs.

"No," he says, "put it here." And he reaches between

34

us, takes my fingers, places them on his chest. His heart pulses beneath my hand.

He inches closer, so we are pressed together, begins to kiss my cheeks. "Maybe you can dump those others and make it just us," he says.

I try to back away. He tenses his grip around me. His heart beats through his skin, pumps heat into my palm. My own heart is on the other side of my hand. I can't feel it through all the clothes.

The wind picks up. Cold air slips between us, sweeps down both sides of my hand.

"Stay with me," he says. "I know this place, we can do it inside. It's got a bed. You could sleep over at night. We could have coffee there in the morning."

No, I want to say. I go to open my mouth and then I start to shiver, everywhere, my whole body. I can't control it. Like it has a mind of its own.

He pulls me tighter than ever. So tight, I feel like he's moved inside me.

The wind keeps gusting. I can't stop shivering. "I'm so cold," I whisper. The words tremble through my lips.

"Just lie here," he says, and he blows a long puff of breath onto my cheek. It's soft where it hits my skin. Then he tilts his head slightly, and does it again, this time on my temple. He does this over and over. He rings my face with his breath.

I am warm under it. But my skin chills as soon as he inhales again, as soon as he moves on to the next spot. "Do you like this?" he asks between breaths.

"I don't know," I say.

He lowers his head and exhales right onto my lips. It is a large, full, strong surge of air. It shoots veins of warmth into the rest of my face. I close my eyes. "Yes," I say. "This feels good."

I want him to breathe over my whole head. I want him

to breathe over my whole body. It feels so good, so warm, I worry I won't be able to shake him off and walk away.

"Stop," I say. "I can't stay here forever."

"Yes you can," he says. He feels between us for my free hand, the one not on his chest. He finds it and draws it to his mouth and breathes onto the fingers. We are so close, the breath that passes between my fingers falls onto my lips. I open my mouth. The warm air, his air, steams past my teeth, across my tongue. It flows right inside me. It curls deep into me.

The night is very far away. Something has lifted the wind up, and it is in the trees above us now. I can hear it, but I cannot feel it. It does not touch the two of us down here. It does not get near us at all.

THE
GREATEST MYSTERY
OF THEM ALL

MY MOTHER SHOT ME TO DEATH last night. I was trying to keep her from going on a drug run, but she insisted. "It's just this once," she said, buttoning a purple blazer over her orange stretch pants. "Ha! You think I'm an idiot?" I said. "I know you've been doing this for ages. But this time is more dangerous — I can feel it. Please don't go."

I started crying. I thought she'd respond to tears; mothers usually do. For the first time in my fourteen years, I felt desperate. I'd do anything to stop her: cling to the cuff of her pants as she marched out the door; call the police.

I guess she knew that. But my mother is not a woman to be deterred.

So when I grabbed her and hugged her tight to say good-bye, planning as I felt her large breasts pressing into me how I would turn her in just to stop her, she pulled out a pistol and shot me four times in the stomach.

I stumbled backward and looked at her. She was calm as she fitted the pistol into her pocket, the same one where she kept her Kleenex and Chap Stick. I was stunned but I wasn't angry. I knew she did what she felt she had to do. I said, "See you in Heaven," because I had a feeling that she was going to die soon. She said, "Jews don't believe in Heaven."

She was holding me in her arms, and I could feel her love for me. Then I faded into death.

In Heaven my grandfather found me the first day at a corner playground. I was shooting baskets by myself. Here they let you look any way you wanted. I'd chosen to become a slender blonde with a little button nose and perfect white teeth. But Grandpa had stayed the same: short, round, and bald, still hunched over from the years in his tailor shop. He wore a yarmulke, like all the other men I'd seen.

"Your mother," he said to me after we'd hugged each other. "She's up to no good down there."

"I know," I said. "She's how I got here in the first place."

"Nice here, isn't it? No roaches. No rent."

"I didn't think Jews lived after death," I said.

"Az men lebt, derlebt men zich alts," he said, shrugging. "If you live long enough, you will live to see everything."

I never told the neighbors that my mother dealt drugs. "Oh, not *her,*" they'd have said, laughing. My mother was known for baking the best gingersnap cookies on our block. Also, she made excellent whitefish, and always got all the bones out. After school she and I would sit down and watch TV. My mother liked old movies best. Sometimes she'd get a call during a show and would have to leave the room, and then I'd change the channel to reruns of *I Dream of Jeannie.* All the while I could hear her down the hall, mumbling things like, "Is the recipe right?" and "Well, taste some of it, then!" I'd seen those callers when they pulled up to our house at night in what looked like normal pizza delivery trucks. Tall men with beard stubble and cigarette butts hanging from their lower lips. They'd do their transactions on the porch. She'd turn off the Chinese lanterns and slip the contraband into the metal credenza where she stored the badminton set.

I watched from my window. My mother is not as she appears, I wanted to tell my neighbors. But I knew they would laugh me off. And what difference would it make to them anyway? *They* wouldn't be affected by her actions.

There are places up here where you can find windows in the ground. They take the place of manholes. If you want, you can look through them and see what's going on below.

My mother is now on a ship in the middle of a vast blue ocean, streaming toward some unknown destination. At her side she fingers the barrel of an Uzi submachine gun. She is still wearing her orange stretch pants, but has changed into a rayon blouse with a pattern of pink flowers splashed across the front. The buttons gap at the apex of her breasts.

Her face is set into that hard look she always got when she told me I had to do something and I tried to resist. Like after the divorce, when she sent me away to that all-summer camp. Or a little later, when she joined a mah-jongg club and insisted that I attend the synagogue youth group. I knew she wasn't playing mah-jongg; she was driving into the city to meet sinister types in back alleys. I could tell because she'd talk jive when she picked me up late at night. "Now, you best do your homework, girl, or you ain't gonna get nowhere, dig?"

Up here I get to meet all my dead relatives. Uncle Saul, who, my mother told me, observed the no-work rule of the Sabbath so strictly that he tore enough toilet paper on Friday afternoons to last him till the evening of the next day. My second cousin Mordecai, who, this again from my mother, lost all his money trying to find a way to make fortune cookies out of matzah. My grandmother, my great-grandparents, cousins — all long dead. They assemble in the Jewish deli on the corner of the street where my apartment is located. Once they get over the way I look — they have all retained their original appearance — they relax and seem pleased to meet me. We sit down and drink cream soda. They pinch my cheek. They speak Yiddish. I do not understand Yiddish. Even death does not change that.

After the divorce, my mother became very strict. Suddenly, every week: Hebrew lessons, meetings with the rabbi, services. "Why do I need to learn all this?" I'd ask, yanking at my stockings on the way to synagogue. "Because our people have been around for thousands of years, and you have a responsibility to carry on the tradition," she would say. I didn't feel any responsibility. I didn't even feel Jewish, except for how I looked and for my limited ability to stumble through the prayer books. I failed every test they gave me. The teacher: "Name four cities in Israel." Me: "Uh, Jerusalem and, uh, uh . . ." The teacher: "Why are blue and white the colors of Judaism?" Me: "——"

The kids at Hebrew school lived in large houses. The girls had their hair done at beauty parlors. The boys discussed politics in the Knesset. Their mothers held bridge parties in the den, their fathers hung PEDIATRICIAN or DENTIST signs outside the entrances to the additions to their ranch houses. Being a Jew meant being like them. My mother and I rented the first floor of a two-family house in a Gentile neighborhood. She was a salesclerk in a five-and-ten. We dressed in remainders from end-of-the-season sales.

At Hebrew school, the other kids would compete to answer the teacher's questions. Me, I'd sit in the corner, staring out the window across the room, stewing about my mother's freedom. She could go anywhere she pleased. She could hang out with bums, if she chose. She could become a drug runner.

In Heaven I go to visit God, but He is not presiding on a throne, the way I'd expected. Here there are different versions of Him, one to a neighborhood. Our God is a butcher. He stands behind a glass counter, taking orders for kosher meat. "How can I help you?" He bellows when I hand Him the ticket with my number.

"I feel so alone here," I say. "Not that I had flocks of friends down on Earth. But here I don't have anyone."

"You have your grandfather, and all your relatives."

"But their lives were so different from mine. We have nothing in common."

He leans back and places His hands on the counter. "What would you like me to do?"

I roll a few ideas around in my head. "Find me a way to occupy my time."

"Do you feel that's the answer?"

"Yes."

"Fine, if that's what you wish. A few blocks from here is a library, and in it are books that will tell you about anything in history. Go ahead. They're in English. That should keep you busy for a while."

What I like about Heaven is that I can learn all the mysteries of the cosmos. Like how evolution *really* works, and what religion — if any — is right, and if there is life on other planets. They are big questions, but actually they have little answers, and once you've learned them, there's not much left to think about except the details. It gets kind of boring, with all this certainty. That's what I *don't* like about Heaven. There is nothing left to wonder about.

I am watching my mother through the manhole. She is lying on a huge, round bed. Portholes look out onto the ocean. Beside her sits an Arab with a black-and-white checkered cloth hanging from his cap. The cloth covers the back of his head and neck like a curtain. I am surprised she is with an Arab, given that she always said they were crazy. She and the Arab are watching *Wheel of Fortune* on the television across the room.

The Arab screws up his face in confusion. "Send me? Send my?"

My mother says, "Send my regards to Broadway." She sighs.

"You are so smart, my little Ernestine," the Arab says. He is smoking a fat cigar. The ashes are falling onto the sheets. I cannot believe my eyes. My mother does not wipe the ashes off or slide an ashtray under the Arab's chin, though she wouldn't even let me eat gingersnaps in the living room without a plate and napkin. I cannot understand it. Evolution and the universe are big questions, but my mother is the greatest mystery of them all.

I used to wonder about Heaven. Even though my mother didn't believe in it. Could Heaven be full of harps and mist and good-looking people wearing white robes? Did it hurt to have the wings put on? Or was Heaven more like a bop on the head — one quick thunk and then you're nothing? I admit I liked the uncertainty. Why read a whole book if you already know the ending?

My grandfather tells me he cannot understand my mother's behavior. "She was such a good girl. She studied Hebrew. She did her lessons at regular school. Once she got married, she was not so good at keeping the Sabbath, and she did neglect your religious education. But still, she had a kind heart."

"She's very good at acting," I tell him. "The neighbors and the rabbi thought she was a model mother."

"Where's your father?" he says.

"Haven't you been watching? Three years ago he left her for a lady professor. That's when my mother started making me go to synagogue. That's also when she started dating.

The men were OK at first, guys who owned companies and did things like take me to ball games. But sooner or later, something would go wrong and she'd be alone again. She'd cry for a few weeks, then drag herself back out. After a while, I guess she lost her heart. First she took up with a bartender. Then it was an ex-con with a betting habit. And then a coke dealer who carried around the phone numbers of hit men in his wallet. And all the time she kept signing me up for more religious school activities."

"Have you told your father about this?"

"He said I could stay with him for a weekend, if I really needed to. I told him I'd try to stick it out. I didn't think things would get as bad as they did."

The Arab is my mother's lover. That much is for sure. He arranges to have a carton of heavenly hash ice cream parachuted onto the ship. He never takes off the hat with the veil, not even in bed or in the shower.

From up here, you can see people down there doing everything. Using the bathroom, fooling around in bed, picking their noses. You get used to it after a while. Maybe even begin to enjoy it.

We don't do much of anything up here. The books are boring once you've read a few of them. And my relatives spend their time gossiping about people from their past. All I can make out are phrases like "Finkelstein! Ach! *Der mensch iz meshugge!*" I go for walks and it's the same thing: people sitting around, eating fatty Jewish food, speaking Yiddish. They glance at me, with my new photogenic looks, and pause for a second, as if trying to place me. Then they wave their hands, and turn away.

On Earth I used to watch the models in commercials. They were all five feet eight with teaspoon breasts and teeth that had been blessed by an orthodontist. I made notes about them on a pad I kept on a shelf above the TV. I ate through boxes of pretzels and cans of macaroons as I followed the models' careers.

Before I went to bed I'd stand in front of my mirror. Face front. Turn to the right. The proportions were all off, and the shadows from my nose buried half my face in darkness. I would think of my mother's line: "If a girl has no other virtues, even a freckle can be considered one." I would scrutinize my reflection for a freckle. But even that, I could not find.

My mother's ship docks somewhere in Asia. The bay is cramped with small fishing canoes and ramshackle houseboats. Some people in the houseboats are leaning over the sides to scrub their clothes, while others stand on the decks and empty baskets of garbage into the water. My mother steps down the ramp in her green wraparound skirt and white blouse with the big bow on the collar. The Arab is at her side.

Little Asian children swarm around my mother. She smiles at them and walks across the docks and into the streets of the city.

In every doorway, people are selling their wares: vegetables, fish, shoes, dresses. My mother and her lover pay no attention as the merchants call out to them. She and the Arab stride with a sense of purpose. Children skip behind them.

When my mother reaches a white house with one side settled lower into the ground than the other, she turns and addresses the little ones who are following. "Children," she says, "you will have to leave us now. I have things I must do."

One of the larger children translates for the others. A few of them cry, but they all walk away. My mother and her lover enter the house.

★

My grandfather is squatting beside me over the window. Company is something I never had before, when I looked out my window, waiting for my mother to come home from her dates. "I don't know what I did wrong," my grandfather says. Neither do I. I am wondering how she got into drug running at all. Of all the hobbies she could have chosen, why this one? If she wanted excitement, she could have put food coloring in her cake batter. She could have taken up smoking. Or even read dirty novels from the library. But no. She had to go in for danger.

Inside the sinking Asian house is a huge room. It is filled with delicate plants and there are pillows on the floor.

"Look at this place," my mother says to the Arab. "Look at this mess. These people should put their things away the minute they walk in the door, not just drop them wherever they please."

The Arab lifts the lids of several tin boxes that are lying on the pillows. Inside each box is a colored powder, each a different shade of white or brown. He stuffs his pockets with the powder. His jacket bulges, and powder flurries down his front like snow.

At the far end of the room, two Asian men appear with a large scale, the kind you use to weigh meat. "I'll take two hundred and thirty-five pounds," my mother calls out. She walks up to them. I think it humorous that she chose that number, as it used to be our address. When she gets close, she pulls out her pistol. "And keep your thumb off the scale. I've got my eye on you."

One time my mother discovered me watching the neighbors. "How could you do that?" she said. "It's rude."

"It's only rude if they find out," I said.

"But there's so much around here for you to do. I bought you that microscope you've been asking for, and you've

47

got your Hebrew lessons, and of course there's your regular homework. You shouldn't waste your time spying on other people."

"I wouldn't have to spy on them if I could go out and be with them."

"During the day, dear, not at night."

"But all I can do at night is watch the neighbors or TV."

"Or do your homework."

"I'd rather go out."

"I want you where I know you'll be safe until I get home from my dates." She said this in a voice as sweet as syrup, and pulled the curtains shut.

My mother makes the two men wrap each pound of powder individually. Then she has the entire shipment loaded into Acme shopping bags. The men make a series of phone calls, and in no time a squadron of tough-looking boys appears at the door. The men hand each boy a bag.

"Now, don't dawdle," my mother tells them. "I must get back to the ship by lunch."

The boys nod and whisper to each other in Asian.

Some people have joined Grandpa and me at the window. "This is a pretty good show," they say. "Who is it?"

"My mother," I say.

"Mothers," says one of them. "My mother shipped me off to a military academy when I was seven."

"That's nothing," another says. "Mine ran away one night and didn't get in touch with us for eleven years."

"Your mothers really did that?" I ask.

"Yes," the first one says.

"You just can't make sense of mothers," the other one adds.

I think about this. During my life — well, until the last year — my mother kept the house clean and the refrigerator stocked. She always sewed my Halloween costume from scratch and dressed me every morning during those months in fourth grade when my arm was broken. She was a great cook. She never bothered me about my weight. And at dinner every night she asked me how my day had gone, and really listened when I talked, and then told me how her day had gone, too, if I thought to ask.

Maybe my mother was not so bad. Maybe, for whatever reason, she just fell apart. I would have to give this possibility some consideration.

The crew of my mother's ship lifts anchor, and the ship pulls out of port. My mother and her lover flutter down to their bedroom.

"I do so love helping Third World economies," my mother says, flopping onto the round bed. She leans against some pillows and clicks on the television with the remote control. *Dallas* is on. J.R. looks into the camera and says, *"Hi choi, enki gen sheh, Bobby."*

I realize I have seen this episode before, so I get up and walk to a shop on the corner. Through the plate glass window I observe stout young girls gathered around a seamstress, trying on bridal gowns. They suck in their stomachs and stand before the mirror. The seamstress opens her hands, palms up. "So, we can alter it," I hear her say through the glass.

I step in closer, until I can look at myself reflected in the plate glass of the bridal shop. My new blond hair is so well coiffed it seems dipped in glue. I touch my full, rosy lips, rest my slender fingers beside my watery blue eyes. Inside, I feel the same. But outside it's wrong. This is a perfect face. It has never been slapped by truth.

I go to God the Butcher and tell Him I want to look like myself again. Back to hips, breasts, nose, and belly. A body built to bear babies. He slices me some corned beef — my mother's favorite meal. "Cook it up with some of this," He says, handing me a jar filled with hyssop. "Then eat it. All of it. That should do the trick."

I go home carrying my corned beef, wondering if I've ever heard of cold cuts being cooked with hyssop. On the way I see Grandpa leaning over our manhole. He glances at me.

"I think your mother's on her way up here," he says. "She's about to get it from some drug pirates."

I scramble over to join him. My mother is standing on her deck, facing a pair of thugs with pronounced underbites. "You're bluffing," my mother says. She begins to turn away. One of the thugs whips out a gun and pulls the trigger. My mother crumples to the deck before she can show fear or surprise.

"Well, that's a shame," Grandpa says, rising to his feet. "But I want you to remember this: *A shlechteh mameh iz nish-tu.* There is no such thing as a bad mother."

"How can you say that, given what she did to me?" I ask.

"Bad acts do not necessarily make someone a bad person," he says.

I stand over my frying pan. The corned beef sizzles below me. Outside, on the street, I see God the Butcher talking to my mother. She looks the same except she teeters a little, as if she's dizzy. Dying, she'll discover, isn't so bad, but death itself is boring. I'm sure this is not how she thought it would turn out.

As I fork the meat onto a plate, I am surprised to realize I am getting excited by her arrival. I walk into the living room, pull up a chair so I can see out the window, and sit down with my plate. Then I start chewing the food, slowly, watching them talk on the street. It's after midnight, but that's all right. I'll wait up for her till dawn if I have to. I don't mind. I want to be here when she gets in, so I can hug her hello, and tell her I'm OK. And let her see how much she's worried me. And finally give her a piece of my mind.

TRAINS

A YOUNG COUPLE is dancing on a stoop. The boy, who wears headphones, pumps his arms and skips about in time to music only he can hear. The girl, who watches him as if he were a spotlight, sways back and forth in silence, her movements complementing his. She cannot hear a sound. She follows the rhythm of his body. I smile up at them as I walk by. This must be love.

My new boyfriend says that he was sexually initiated at age eight. At the time, his mother was "sick," either getting addicted to pain killers in the hospital or withdrawing from those same pain killers in detox. He was home from boarding school for the weekend. The only other person in the house was the maid, Annabel.

Annabel was a stout, mildly retarded woman with flesh-colored hair. I imagine she had mongoloid features, though my boyfriend has never said this. Still, I see her eyes slanting toward the ground, her boxy head, her watermelon grin.

That afternoon, she was sweeping the hallway. He was in his bedroom, reading train magazines. He loves trains. The first time he rode one, which was also the first time he visited his mother in the hospital, he decided he liked trains better than people. That was because trains are powerful and hold you securely inside themselves. Sometimes, when I walk home alone after our dates, I think he still feels this way, and I wonder, as I've wondered about other things with other men, what I can do about it.

It was a late afternoon in the fall. Only a sliver of sunlight crept into his room from the westward window in the hall-way.

He got up and walked to that window; to this day, he does not remember why. Annabel was holding the broom. She brushed her hair off her forehead and said, "Sad your mom's gone?"

"Yes," he said, and looked out the window. He remembers a band of red running across the horizon like a trail of blood and the silhouettes of trees stretching like a dozen empty arms into the clouds.

Then he turned. Annabel was resting the broom against the wall. She stepped over, put out her arms, and hugged him.

They did not kiss or make love. They did not even take off their clothes. All they did was hold each other and roll around the hallway like tumbleweeds, first in silence, then in laughter.

This is why, he warned me at the beginning, he is attracted to chunky women. He warned me because I am a size five, four feet eleven inches tall. He said he likes me all right, and he'll hang out with me if I want, but I must understand that his most erotic fantasy is to live on a bed in the back of a roadside diner that only serves fat women truck drivers.

I try to understand him, why he feels this way. I try to be sensitive. This is what men like in women.

Like last month, when I talked him into coming to my apartment. After dinner, I stripped off my dress and lay on my bed and called him over. He shuffled across the room and sat at the edge of the blanket. With my small fingers,

I reached up and began to unbutton his shirt. He shivered before I had opened it enough to see any chest hair. So I stopped. I said maybe we should go for a walk instead. As soon as we stepped onto the street, I knew he was grateful, and I could feel that he liked me more than ever.

Last night too. That was when I finally got some of his clothes off.

We went to his room for the first time. He lives across the street from a bus station and a sexual aids store. His single room is empty except for a foam mattress and a folding card table. Its only window is large and dirty and has no curtains.

We sat on the floor. He bent his legs in front of him like an upside-down V and told me to do the same. Then he pulled me close and clamped my legs between his knees, so everything from my ankles to my thighs was pressed together. I glanced out the window and saw businessmen furtively shoving packages of sexual aids inside their jackets, adolescent prostitutes calling to them from the corner, anxious tourists walking head down along the gutter edge of the sidewalk. No one looked up at us.

I closed my eyes for a moment. Suddenly I felt like he and I were riding a train together, and we were the only passengers. I wondered if he would be able to hear me when I talked, or if the train was clattering so loudly as it rushed along the tracks that he could not.

He unzipped his pants. He told me to stay dressed. Then he rubbed himself very delicately against my tightly squeezed shins. The motion was so slight, I thought he was sitting still.

When he was done, I tried to touch him, but he whispered that since this was our first time, he wanted things to be perfect. I did not understand but said that I did. It was our first time together. I wanted things to be perfect, too.

TWINS

THEY CAME on a Thursday. There were two of them, two girls, and someone told Brenda they were sisters. Brenda was confused about how that could be. She had a sister, and the two of them were girls, but Brenda and her sister didn't look like Ramona and Remmie. Brenda and her sister were their own selves.

Not Ramona and Remmie. When you got one, you got the other, like prickers on a rose. Ramona was the one with legs that worked. She had brown hair and blue eyes and she looked pretty normal, except that Remmie grew out of her chest. Remmie was cuter than Ramona, but she was smaller, and her legs looked like mashed potatoes, and were probably about as easy to walk on. Ramona had to carry her everywhere.

It was a Thursday when Ramona and Remmie first came to Horizons. That's the place where all the special people in town — people like Brenda — went to work every day. There they did jobs like make boxes and paste on labels: "Things that help out people in the post office or large companies somewhere," Brenda's mom once explained to her. On Thursdays Brenda stuffed her week's load of envelopes into boxes. She liked that better than the jobs she did on other days because it was easy. She didn't have to worry she'd do it wrong and get her supervisor angry.

One of the bosses let Ramona and Remmie into the workroom. "We Are the World" was playing on the radio, and Brenda's buddy Edgar was singing along. It was his favorite song. Edgar wasn't too handsome — he was tall and fat, and when he worked he forgot to swallow and his chin got wet — but he was nice. He was trying so hard to get the words right on that song and paste his labels on straight that he didn't even notice them come in.

Brenda watched them go across the room and walk up to an empty table. Ramona sat down on the bench and put Remmie on the table in front of her, real gentle, like she was putting down a big dish. They both wore shirts that were bunched up around their chests, and the bunch on Ramona's shirt was pressed up against the one on Remmie's shirt. They sat close together.

Edgar looked over their way. His tongue was sticking out like it always did when he took note of something. Brenda looked around and saw everybody else was checking them out. Even Lisa Cumbermiller, and she never noticed anything except her work and her lunch and her cigarettes. She even ignored her clothes — her bra straps always showed. But these girls were something Lisa couldn't ignore.

Brenda wanted to look too — they were so strange — and then this little voice popped into her head. It said, "Don't stare. It's not nice." Usually Brenda heard voices saying that whenever she went out shopping. Not voices in her head, like Ritchie Vailer said he heard. But voices from people around her. It used to get to her when she was little, and she'd be in the Shop-Rite with her mom, and other moms would say it to their kids. "Don't stare." It used to make her cry. Her mom had to take her out and put her in the car and talk to her till she calmed down. But now she was used to it. She was grown up. Now she thought "Don't stare" was a polite thing to say.

So Brenda went back to work. She heard the supervisor explain things to the girls, like when they stopped for lunch and that there was no fighting over the radio and what kinds of jobs they'd do. He said that most of them on Brenda's part of the floor did labels and envelopes, and the girls would be sorting labels today. The girls talked to him. Brenda couldn't make out what they were saying but she figured the words were real and made sense, because the supervisor didn't say "What?" or tell Edgar to turn down the radio so he could hear better. Then he gave them a tray of labels and told them to sort by letter.

Brenda never sorted by letter. When she first came to Horizons three years ago, they taught her to sort labels by color. She was too old for school anymore, and her mom felt bad about Brenda sitting around the house by herself all day long, going out only when she walked the dogs or worked in the garden. The labels were tough at the beginning; Brenda kept picking up two or three at a time and not even knowing it. But finally she got it down, she did a whole box perfectly. Her mom told everyone on the block. She called Brenda's sister, Ellie. Ellie didn't need to live at home like Brenda did. A week later Brenda got a letter from her. Her mom read it to Brenda. It said, "Congratulations on your new success. I bet you feel so grown up. Now you can start being more independent."

After the supervisor walked away, no one talked for a long time, so Brenda could tell that everybody was still watching the girls. She tried to keep her mind on the radio, but the man who talked on it thought he was better than everyone else; he put anyone not like him down and acted like it was funny. Sometimes people at Horizons laughed along, but Brenda never saw the joke. So instead she listened for whether these girls talked, and once in a while she'd look up to see what they were doing. They were working, like everyone else. Brenda passed them when she went to the bathroom and checked out the bunch on their shirts; maybe there'd be a hole and she could see what was going on underneath. But there wasn't a hole. And then when she was in the bathroom she wondered how they did *that*.

By the time lunch rolled around, everyone had started to talk again. Some of them talked about TV from Wednesday night, but a lot of them talked about the girls. Brenda could hear them. They said, "Wonder if they're people," and other things like that. Nothing Brenda cared to remember.

At lunch, the girls sat off in a corner by themselves. No one went over to them or sat at the tables nearby. And Brenda wasn't going to either. She sat at the same table every day, with Marty and Edgar.

Marty was one of the only black people at Horizons or in the whole town, even. He worked with the broom-and-mop guys upstairs. They came to work later than anyone else and stayed till after dark, so they could clean up the place before the next day. Sometimes they'd go on trips to clean churches, and they'd get to meet the priest there and shake his hand. Marty was skinny and his hair was cut short. He wasn't bad-looking except for how yellow his teeth were.

Brenda pulled out her sandwich and looked over to those girls. "What do you think's going on with them?" she asked. They were sitting with their heads bent close together and weren't looking into the room at all.

"Ain't got a clue," Marty said.

Edgar just rested his head in his hands and looked their way. "They's pretty," he said.

"Yeah," Brenda said. "Pretty as people on TV."

"They're weird," Marty said. "The Devil makes rats prettier'n them."

Brenda had seen rats a few times in books, and they sure didn't look like those girls. But there was no use arguing with Marty. He stuck to his guns when he made up his mind about something. Brenda bit into her tuna fish sandwich. She wondered if the girls ate tuna fish.

Then Lisa Cumbermiller came over, pushing a chair in front of her. "Those twinkies stole my place," she said, pulling the chair up to Brenda's table and plopping down into it. It was the first time she'd ever talked to them. Her bra strap was sticking out, and it looked like she'd never thrown it in the wash.

Brenda said, "We don't mind if you sit with us."

"I do," Marty said, and he shot Brenda this look.

Lisa Cumbermiller put her lunch box on the table and pulled out three sandwiches, two bags of Cheese Doodles, two Cokes, and a fudge brownie.

"Why you eating so much?" Marty asked. "You fat enough already."

"That's not nice," Edgar said. He stuck his elbow into Marty's side. Edgar knew good manners. He always said thank you when the supervisors gave him work.

Once, when Horizons took the whole work crew on a picnic, a group of kids stood in the bushes and shouted things at them, calling them "retards" and "half-brains" and making sounds like they were monkeys. After a while, the kids rode their bikes off to the next field and started playing ball. Later on, they hit the ball so hard, it rolled clear over to the picnic. No one from Horizons wanted to get near it except Edgar. He just picked it up and carried it across the field to them. The kids asked him to stay. He said no and thanked them for asking. They followed him all the way back to the picnic and kept asking him over and over, and he didn't even cry. He just kept saying, "No thank you, no thank you," till the counselors got up and made the kids leave.

Lisa chomped down on a sandwich. "I'm not fat," she said. "I'm gonna have a baby."

Marty sat up taller. "Then why you working? Ladies who gonna have babies should stay home in bed."

"Not me. I can do whatever I want since I'm not keeping it."

Brenda had always wanted a baby, but her mom said they need to depend on you too much so she shouldn't even think about it. "Why aren't you going to keep it?" she asked.

Lisa stuffed in half a sandwich and said with her mouth full, "It'll have something wrong. I bet it will."

"How do you know that?" Brenda asked. "You can't know that."

"Yes I can. I'm going to see my doctor and he'll put a pin in my stomach to see if anything funny's going on."

Brenda said, "What if they find something wrong?"

"They'll take it out so I won't have it."

That made Brenda lean back and think. She wondered what kind of thing could be so wrong that they'd have to take the baby out of Lisa.

They sat and chewed on their food. Marty finished before the rest of them and burped. Then he said, "My mama keep saying we might move back to where she from."

"Why does she want to do that?" Brenda asked.

"She say she don't want my sisters marrying white men. And the two in high school, only boys they talk about is white boys. She worried about them, and the younger ones too."

"You can't move," Brenda said. "You're our friend."

Edgar looked like he might cry. "We won't be able to eat lunch with you if you go."

"She say, 'The world be a better place if people stayed with they own kinds.' And sometime, like when we shopping in town and everybody be white and walking around us and holding they bags close, I think she right."

Brenda pointed across the room. "What about them? We're not their type."

Marty nodded. "That's right. And they shouldn't be here."

"What are they, anyway?" Brenda said.

Lisa Cumbermiller scrunched up a Cheese Doodles bag. "They're twins. I heard the supervisors talking."

"They not twins," Marty said. "They don't look like each other. Look at that little one. She look like pot cheese."

"Twins don't have to look the same," Lisa said.

That was news to Brenda. All the twins she saw on TV and in stores looked just like each other. If one had legs, the other did too. Even their clothes matched and their hair was done the same. But not these girls. Ramona had on a brown dress and wore a ponytail. Remmie had on a pink dress, and her hair was curly and long and she had bangs. Brenda didn't see how they could be twins. And stuck togeher like that too.

But she didn't ask questions. She just worked on her sandwich. After all, Lisa was pregnant, so Brenda guessed she was an expert on babies. She guessed Lisa knew about things like twins.

After work Brenda took the Horizons van to her house. She could hardly wait for her mom to get home so she could tell her about Ramona and Remmie. They didn't ride with the rest of the Horizons people. Their dad picked them up. He looked just like other dads.

At home Brenda did like she always did. First she walked the dogs. She really liked dogs, especially dogs with papers. She took care of four every day after work. The dog owners were different from most of the people who lived near her — they said hi if they saw her. The other neighbors just weren't friendly. They usually didn't even look Brenda's way when she passed by. Except for the kids. Sometimes after dinner, Brenda would turn off the lights in the living room so no one outside could see her, and she'd look out the window and watch the kids playing in the street. They would say mean things to each other, but never as mean as what they said to Brenda.

When she got home from walking the dogs, Brenda went out back to work in her garden. That's how she learned to read — her mom put sticks in the ground with letters for each plant so Brenda would know what was coming up. Sometimes she wished her mom had put up whole words because maybe then Brenda would have learned how to read more than just letters. It didn't matter, really. She did what she liked without having to read. And she liked gardens. The thing she liked best about them was making a plan and then watching it happen just like you wanted it to. As long as you were careful, it always turned out right.

That day her mom got home while Brenda was still in the garden. Brenda knew she was there when she smelled hot dogs. She went inside and washed up and came to the table.

Her mom passed Brenda a roll. "Any sign of the carrots yet?"

"Just a little," Brenda said. "They like to hide away from everything else."

Brenda's mom put a hot dog on Brenda's roll. "I hope they come up soon. I told the people at work I'd bring some in."

"Don't they have gardens, too?"

"A lot of them do, but the vegetables from yours come

out especially delicious. You take such good care, every-thing's so neat and evenly spaced."

There was a while when her mom didn't pay so much attention to Brenda. That was because her mom used to need to sleep a lot; she'd come home from work and just conk out. Brenda guessed she was unhappy. But just before Brenda began at Horizons, her mom started staying up till bedtime and taking note of what Brenda did. Like Brenda had always forgotten when her period was coming and what to do when she got it. Her mom didn't care for a long time. Then when the Horizons people called and said Brenda could start in a month, her mom said she should learn. Her mom got a doll and fed it red water and made Brenda practice helping the doll till she got good at it. Now, Brenda can even figure out when she'll get it and how much napkin stuff she'll need for the day. Her mom calls her an expert.

Brenda sat down to start eating, but before she picked up her fork she said, "Mom, we got these new people at Horizons today. Lisa Cumbermiller says they're twins. They're, like, stuck together" — she tapped her chest — "here."

Her mom stared at Brenda for a second. "Do they look the same?"

"Sort of. They're both cute and got the same color hair and eyes. But one can't walk. The other one holds her."

At first her mom looked like she didn't understand. Brenda wondered if she'd messed up her words again. She hadn't done that in a long time.

"Oh," her mom said suddenly, "they're Siamese twins. I saw them in the paper."

"What's that?"

"They're like regular twins, except when they were inside their mother they never split apart into two independent people."

69

Brenda said, "I've never seen anything like that before."

"That's because there aren't many of them. And this pair at Horizons, well, they're extra-unusual, even for Siamese twins."

"One's got funny legs."

"I know. In the newspaper they said that one of these girls didn't grow right, and that the other one has to carry her around."

Brenda wondered if Lisa Cumbermiller's baby wasn't growing right. Maybe it had bad legs too, or a bad head. She said, "If I'd been like that, would you of gotten rid of me before I was born?"

"How can you even ask me that?" her mom said. "You're my baby and I love you, no matter what."

"Well, Lisa Cumbermiller thinks she'll get rid of her baby if something's wrong."

"That's Lisa. I wouldn't do that."

Brenda bit into her hot dog and chewed for a minute. Then she asked, "Mom, can Siamese twins come apart?"

"I don't think so, most of the time. I think they usually share something too important. Like their stomachs, maybe."

Brenda considered that. Since the other person had to eat too, and there'd be only one stomach between them, Brenda would have less space for food than she had now. That didn't sound so good.

"Why don't you talk to them?" her mom asked.

"I don't know," Brenda said. "It'd be weird. I wouldn't know which one to talk to. I wouldn't know what to say. Anyway, I have all the friends I need. I was just wondering, that's all."

After that first day, Brenda tried not to stare at Ramona and Remmie. She'd look their way every time a new song came on the radio, but that was just to see if they liked it. Only they never noticed the songs. All they did was talk to each other, real low and quiet. Sometimes they'd laugh and shake their heads. Brenda couldn't hear their words. Ramona did the label work and Remmie looked on. Everyone except Brenda and Edgar kept their eyes on the twins as if they were watching a TV set.

At night Brenda talked to the dogs. She asked them if it was OK to act like nothing had changed at Horizons. She asked them if she was doing the right thing. Ramona and Remmie didn't seem lonely, so she didn't *have* to talk to them. But for some reason she began to want to. Maybe it was because they wore pretty dresses and smelled like flowers. She didn't know. But she didn't do anything, and the days kept passing and passing, and she just felt a little worse all the time.

Time went fast that summer, faster than Brenda had ever remembered it going. And a lot seemed to happen. The biggest thing was that Marty and his family moved away to Detroit. Brenda didn't even get a chance to buy him a present.

She cried when he got off the van that last day. So did Edgar. He leaned across the van seat, and they waved bye to Marty out the window. After they drove away, Edgar told Brenda that Marty used to help him in the bathroom. She asked who'd help him now, and he said no one. He said he just wouldn't tuck in his shirt so you couldn't tell that his pants were unzipped. Brenda told him she'd help if she could, but she couldn't because she was a girl.

Around that same time Lisa Cumbermiller got rid of her baby. She told them all at lunch, even though they didn't want to hear about it. She said it happened fast and was hardly sloppy at all. She laughed. Brenda threw her lunch in the garbage when she told them. The next day Lisa Cumbermiller moved away from their table so she could sit with the other fat ladies at Horizons. Good, Brenda thought. Let them stuff their faces together.

Then one of the little kids on Brenda's block fell off his bike and broke his head open. She saw it happen from the living room window, the ambulance taking him away and everyone in his family crying. A week later they brought him home with a big white towel wrapped around his head. He didn't look the same. And whenever Brenda saw his mother, she'd be crying. Soon she began calling Brenda's mom every night. They'd never spoken before this, and now it was like they were best friends. They'd talk a long time, and Brenda's mom would make a mess of the kitchen. After they hung up, the table would be full of fat books that didn't have any pictures, only letters and drawings of bent-up black lines that made Brenda think of lightning.

Brenda's garden did real well that summer. She kept the rows neat and tidy. She cleaned out the weeds every day, sprayed the plants with a hose when the ground got dry. Her mom said it was the best garden she'd ever grown and sent a picture of it to Ellie. Ellie wrote back and said it looked like Brenda knew what she was doing and that maybe she should go work at a real place, like the Shop-Rite, so she could make enough money to move out on her own. Brenda's mom shook her head when she read that. The whole idea sounded strange to Brenda, since she'd never seen gardens growing in the Shop-Rite. But who knew what it was like where Ellie lived.

In the fall a terrible flu came around. Brenda's mom said walking the dogs made her as healthy as a St. Bernard, and she must have been right, because Brenda didn't get it. But her mom did. She missed three days of work.

At Horizons, people started dropping all around Brenda. Poor Edgar got it so bad he had to go into the hospital. The counselors called a special class and told them ways to fight it off. They said they should try extra hard because the sort of people who work at Horizons get sicker than most people. But it didn't help much. Every day fewer and fewer people came in.

Brenda thought about Edgar and Marty all the time; she missed them something awful. Her mom let her call Marty once, and then wrote his name on envelopes so Brenda could mail him some of her pictures. A few days later her mom took Brenda to see Edgar in the hospital. Tubes were twisted all over him, and his parents told her he'd filled in eleven coloring books. He could hardly breathe when she saw him. He smiled but when he started coughing, they rushed Brenda out. At lunch every day, she'd think about him.

Pretty soon most everyone got sick from the flu. All over Horizons, all day long, it was quiet. Brenda could even change the radio from that show with the guy she didn't like, because no one who liked him was around. She thought that'd make her feel good, but without Edgar there to be glad with, it didn't much matter.

Finally there were only a few of them left. Brenda, Elise Sandover, Ritchie Vailer, and those twins. Brenda didn't like to eat alone, but she had no choice. Elise made funny burping sounds all the time, and Ritchie's nose was sort of near his ear. And, even though Brenda had been noticing the twins looking her way, she was too scared to ask them to sit with her. She wasn't sure why they were taking note of her — if they wondered whether she had the flu or what. Maybe they were looking because they were jealous that Brenda had a friend, or because she was normal. She didn't have a twin. She was her own person.

So Brenda ate by herself at a table in the corner. There

wasn't much to watch. Just the walls and Elise and Ritchie.

Brenda was hunched over her tuna fish sandwich, humming one of Edgar's favorite songs and thinking about trying to visit him in the hospital again when someone touched her shoulder.

"Can we sit here?" a soft voice said, and Brenda smelled that nice flower smell. She looked up and saw Ramona and Remmie. They'd come over to her! At first she didn't know what to say — no one'd ever come over to her except Lisa Cumbermiller. And Brenda hadn't wanted to talk to her.

"Yeah, sure," Brenda said. She moved her food over so Remmie could sit on the table. After Ramona set her down, Remmie leaned over and spread their lunch out next to her. There were bologna sandwiches and hard-boiled eggs and chocolate milk. Food like Brenda ate.

Remmie's bangs were pinned back with blue and green barrettes that sparkled, and all the rest of her curly hair just hung on her shoulders. Ramona's hair was straight as always. Her ponytail was tied up with purple ribbon. When she sat on the bench, Brenda said, "You two are real beautiful. You should be models."

They looked at each other. "I don't think people who hire models would be too receptive to us," Ramona said.

"I don't know what that means."

Remmie gave Ramona this look, like she'd done something wrong. "She means they might not find us pretty. We're too unusual."

Brenda looked down at her food. She still had half a sandwich left and she didn't know what to say.

"You like dogs?" she asked.

"Yeah," Remmie said, "we have a German shepherd and a very old —"

"Very old mutt," Ramona said. They said "very old" at the same time. Brenda wasn't sure which one to talk to.

She looked from one to the other the way she used to watch her mom and Ellie play Ping-Pong.

"I like dogs that have papers," Brenda said. "They're better-looking that way."

Remmie twirled one of her curls in her fingers and said, "Actually, our mutt is very good-looking."

Ramona said, "Yeah. And in general, pedigree dogs tend to be more neurotic than mixed breeds."

"What's that?"

"Neurotic?" Ramona said, scraping the floor with her feet. "That's when someone's unstable emotionally."

Remmie put her hands flat on the table between her and Ramona, and gave Ramona that look again.

"You mean sick in the head?" Brenda asked.

"No," Remmie said. "Just troubled. Not crazy."

Brenda wondered if her father'd been neurotic. He'd died when she was a baby. Her mom said he drank so much, it was like he was from Mars. "If someone's like that," Brenda asked, "do their kids get it too?"

"Sometimes," Remmie said.

"It's not something you're born with. It's something you acquire," Ramona said.

"She means you become that way."

"Oh," Brenda said. "Did you two become that way?"

Remmie laughed, but Ramona didn't. "No, we were born like this," they said at the same time.

"So you're not neurotic?"

"Oh, I don't know about that," Remmie said, picking up a sandwich that was sitting on the table next to her, and smiled at Ramona.

"Can you ever come apart?" Brenda said. "I don't think I'd like to be stuck to my sister, and I know she wouldn't want to be stuck to me."

"We don't enjoy it," Ramona said.

"But it has to be like this," Remmie said. "If we had an operation to take us apart, I'd probably die. And I'd rather be stuck to Ramona than not be here at all."

Brenda looked over at Ramona. She was picking the crust off the bread from her bologna sandwich.

Brenda couldn't imagine being stuck to anyone. Not even Edgar. What if she was stuck to Lisa Cumbermiller? "You don't have it so good," Brenda said.

Ramona sighed. "Very perceptive," she said, and she looked up in the air away from Brenda and Remmie and ran her fingers through her ponytail like a comb.

Remmie said, "It's not so bad. The only times we have trouble are when I set my hair at night, because the curlers poke Ramona in the face while we sleep. And also when she drinks. I can't stand alcohol. What makes her drunk sometimes makes me sick."

Ramona peeled the top slice of bread off her sandwich, then bit into what was left. "I really hate being like this," she said. "The only thing that's good about it is that I'm never lonely."

Brenda looked around the lunchroom. Elise and Ritchie were gone. "I don't know if I've ever been lonely."

Ramona crossed her legs. "Where's your friend?" she said. "That guy you sit with all the time."

"You mean Edgar? He's sick."

"Well, imagine how you'd feel if he never came back," she said.

Brenda hadn't considered that. She'd just taken it for granted he'd be back. But if he didn't get better, it'd be awful, especially with Marty gone. No one to talk to, no one to eat with, no one to look at when a song she liked came on the radio. It made her think about how her garden looked in the winter, or how she felt in the living room, watching the kids outside. "I don't know what I'd do," Brenda said.

"You'd make new friends," Remmie said. "I bet anyone'd be friends with you. You seem to be very considerate. That's why we wanted to meet you."

That made Brenda's face warm, and she felt like she was in the sun. Then she remembered that her mind was not neat and tidy. "But most people aren't like me," she said.

Ramona said, "So make friends with people who aren't."

Brenda didn't know if she wanted to do that. She didn't know if she could. She put her empty Coke can in her lunch box.

"Girls!" A supervisor shouted into the lunchroom. "Didn't you see the time?"

Brenda felt her cheeks turn red. She'd never been late before. Quick as she could, she packed up her lunch and went back to the workroom.

Brenda worked hard that afternoon so her boss would forget what happened at lunch. But Brenda didn't forget, and she didn't want to. Every time she looked up, she'd see the twins watching her. They weren't just staring, either. They were smiling, Ramona a little, and Remmie a lot.

After she walked the dogs that night, Brenda went out to the garden. The pumpkins were coming up and there was still some squash left, but most everything else was gone. Red and yellow and brown leaves from all over the neighborhood had blown onto the yard and were covering the dirt. Brenda didn't go over to pick them out. She just stood at the edge and looked.

With all the leaves there, the garden didn't look so tidy anymore. But it was kind of nice that way, and Brenda didn't want to clean it up. All she wanted to do was step in just far enough to get some pumpkins. Then she could go to the hospital and bring one to Edgar. She figured he'd really like it. And the lady down the street, the one with the little boy who'd been hurt. She might feel good if Brenda brought her one, too. Her mom would know for sure. Brenda could ask her if it was OK to give pumpkins as presents. And, if she said yes, the first one Brenda would pick would be for the twins. She could bring it to them tomorrow. The prettiest and most perfect-shaped one she could find.

HEARTS

WE THINK MY FATHER will die suddenly. We imagine a
heart attack. He is a fat man, a lover of latkes and blintzes,
who smokes cigarettes and is given to rages of such volume
that my mother, sitting on the sidelines all these years, suf-
fers from eardrum damage.

He frequently brings up his death at family gatherings.
"I want to talk about my will," he says. "You must use the
money to care for your mother. She is not to live in a home."
Then he explains, once again, what each of us will get, how
we should invest it so our mother can avoid taxes, what we
should buy for her. Above all, we are told, we must never
forget that every penny is to be spent on her. I always
reassure him: "I will take care of Mama."

At my birth, he named me Hermina, so his name, Her-
mann, could live on. But I will not be passing it on; I have
never married and, though I date and on rare occasions have
allowed a man to spend the night, I am beyond the age of
childbearing. This angers my father, and is the cause, he
says, of his sporadic chest pains. For years, he has sent me
an unsigned card every Mother's Day. I feel chest pains
then, too.

It has long been understood that I will take my mother

in after my father's death. Early on, my sisters told me they would never allow one person to carry the entire burden. But, as each began to make her own family, I would be told in private: "I have too many other things in my life. And we must think of what is best for her."

When I moved out of the house nine years ago, my father insisted my apartment have two bedrooms. He then furnished the second one for my mother without her knowledge, so that it will be ready and welcoming when the time comes. Sometimes men peer at the closed bedroom door and ask if I have a roommate. "Not yet," I tell them, "but I will." My sisters, married and therefore certain they are wiser than I, tell me that somehow I must want to make men fear entrapment; I make them run.

Following my father's suggestion, I have been lining my shelves and filling my closets with gifts for my mother. He sends me lists of things she has always wanted but he has been too cheap to give her: Eastern European novels, an Israeli *mezuzah,* gilded *Pesach* dishes, embroidered antimacassars, real linen sheets, crystal atomizers.

Given what it costs to pay rent on an apartment in a neighborhood that my father considers safe enough for my mother, I don't have money for luxuries like a car and fancy clothes. My sisters visit reluctantly, and only during the day, when they have little to do. They click their tongues at how long it takes me to get home from work, at the pills on my sweaters, the outdated length of my hems. And when they discovered my stock of gifts for our mother, they shook their heads.

My mother pulled me aside last Saturday while my father was out buying cold cuts and my sisters were playing badminton with their families. "Hermina, I have been doing a lot of thinking," she said, "and I realize that I don't expect you to take care of me when your father dies. Just because we took in your aunt after the war doesn't mean you have such an obligation. She spoke no English. She'd lost all her dignity. I'll go into a home."

"I will not hear of it," I said. "It's my responsibility."

Later in the week, she calls and tells me what she has thought all these years: she does not *want* to live with me. She feels I should have a life of my own. She feels I have wasted too much of it already.

I tell her she is mistaken. We will both be happier if we stay together. "That's what family is for," I say.

There is a silence over the phone, and then she says, "I am going to cash in those bonds your father gets me for my birthdays. I plan to put money down at Merry Heart next week."

"But he will be furious," I remind her.

"I am not going to tell him," she replies.

But he will know, somehow. And it will destroy him. It will destroy her.

When we get off, I walk through the apartment, taking out her gifts, setting them on the table. I sit and look at them and try to figure out how to stop her. I must protect my father. I must respect my mother. The gifts are beautiful, and so elegant. I cannot bear to think about what might become of them. They are nothing I can ever use.

PAINT

HE PAINTS ME.

He lays me down on his drop cloth, dips his brushes into cans of paint, and runs the tip of the bristles up my legs, over my hips. The paint tickles as it goes on, like a fine tongue licking its way up my body. He coats me, front and back. It must be done in a single day, so dust doesn't blur his designs before he raises the curtain that hides me at the university gallery. There, I stand on the pedestal. People walk around me, pointing at the amphibians on my breasts, the starfish on my thighs, the feathers painted in my pubic hair. I focus on the other works that surround me. And whenever he walks near, I focus on him.

The figures on me are not like tattoos, because I can wash them off, and because, over the seven weeks that we are in this show, they will tell a story. For each installment, I will change; it is a show of works in progress, where each week the paintings and sculptures will be one step closer to completion. He thinks of it as similar to a seven-part TV series. I don't; I think of it as the first step.

I am his canvas, his art form, his ticket to fame.

He is my provider.

I am fifteen.

For this first show, he paints shapes, fat clouds of turquoise and lavender outlined in black. He tells me they're amoebas, and shows me a book that describes how amoebas reproduce; they split in half, making a child identical to the parent. You mean there's no men and women? I asked as he painted me. I cannot imagine that. I can, he said.

Now, during the cab ride home from the show, my long white hair and its painted designs sprayed against the back of the seat, I watch him sip wine from his flask. He settles back into the cushion and says, The amoebas are over. What'll I do for the next installment?

You have a whole week, I tell him. Didn't you make a movie once? You can come up with something.

I just hope I can keep up the energy.

I tell him, Look, why not try this, and I pull a scrap of paper and a pen out of his coat pocket and draw creatures I learned about in the amoeba book.

He mulls over my scribble of jellyfish and coral, rubbing his chin. You can do it, I say, You could paint history.

He sighs, turns to me, pats my head. You are the perfect model, he says. Gorgeous. Inspiring.

He leans his pale cheek against the window and gazes out. A stoplight tints his black hair red, making his straight strands look dyed. I curl the ends of my own hair in my fingers, remembering I have only another six weeks with him. After that the show will be over and he won't need me anymore.

He does not know my age. He does not know my past. He does not know that I used to live in another city with my mother, or what I left behind in the streets of my old neighborhood.

In that city, I left behind a pride of boys, clustering in the dark alleys between apartment buildings, in the space where the skeletons of stairs were drawn up high and windows flashed white and blue from the safe world of television. The boys met there and counted their money, smoked dope, laid their weapons on the ground for trade or show.

Girls hid in the apartments above. They knew that the alley was not their world. A girl was afraid to look down from her window in case boy eyes traveled up the side of the building, reading each row of dark glass until they locked onto her face. If she was pretty, the boys would glance at each other and nod. Then she was lost the next time she went out alone.

My mother told me I was too beautiful; she said to stay inside at night. But she went out whenever she pleased, and left me alone. I cannot stand to be alone. So I kept the lights off in my room and hid behind our curtains and looked down; I could see the boys, but they couldn't see me. For months I watched them. Finally I climbed onto my fire escape. You'd better look out, baby, they yelled up. I'm looking, I said, Look out for *me*.

I did not know if my mother was in the arms of an old boyfriend or the bed of a new. I stepped back inside, then skipped down the stairs and into the alley. The boys were at the far end; as I shuffled in from the street all I could see of them were the tips of their cigarettes and joints bobbing in the darkness, all I could hear were their murmurs. In the back of the alley I made them out, boys with fingers hooked into belt straps, blowing ripples of smoke out of their mouths. I faced them with my whole five feet. I was thin enough to be carried off by wind, a David facing Goliath. Hey, I said, I want to join, can a girl join? They looked at each other and said, Only one way a girl can join. I walked up to them. One I grabbed, pulled him to me, slid his hands up my dress. Like this? I said. He kissed me. I leaned against the wall and spread my legs. The bricks dug into my back. All around the boys clapped and hollered. It was a big show and I was the star.

Long as I went outside after that, I didn't have to worry and I didn't have to be alone. They took care of me, let me in on their money and dope, kept a watch out when I passed by other gangs. This worked well, though when some of them, the older ones, the dropouts, pressed me into the bushes behind the school, laid me down in the dirt during lunch, I wondered if I'd keep liking it. I wondered if it'd always leave me feeling safe.

When I shower after our first show, paint flows down my body and swirls into the drain. I turn off the water, and a trace of the images remains on me, as though his creatures are lurking beneath my skin.

In his studio I stand wrapped in a towel, dripping on his drop cloth. A documentary about women in other parts of the world is on the television. It started before I stepped into the shower: pictures of bound feet, elongated heads. The sound was off so I couldn't tell if it hurt to have these things done. I wanted to turn the TV up and find out, but he was sitting right there, so I left to take a shower.

Now, wet and clean, I watch women in black pad through a city street. The veil, he mumbles.

The women look as alike as ants. The only ones who stand out are those with glasses. That last film I worked on, he says in a voice like he's dreaming, was about clothing that hasn't changed for centuries. I did a section on veils.

Do you know how to make them? I ask as I watch the women clutch one end to cover their faces.

Sure.

What did it feel like? What did they say it felt like?

He pauses for a minute. I don't remember. But I could wrap you, if you want to find out.

What — put me in a veil?

If you'd like.

It might make him feel good to show off what he knows, and he needs that. OK, I say.

He switches off the television, then goes to the window and unhooks the navy blue sheet that covers the glass. City light fills the room. Across the street in the junkyard are the silhouettes of cranes and the cars they were hoisting when the yard closed today. The metal dangles high, waiting to fall.

I lay my towel on a chair. He tells me to hold one edge of the sheet, then he walks around me, threading it this way and that. There are different styles, he says, but as far as I know, the piece for the head is always separate. He pauses to scan the room, then scoops up the Indian print cloth that covers his pillow and drapes it over my head and neck.

When he is done, I am covered everywhere except my eyes. I turn to see myself reflected in his window. There is almost nothing left of me at all; with my body hidden this much, I could be anyone. A panic rises in me, and I want to rip the whole thing off. I don't like this, I say. I feel like I'm lost.

Try closing your eyes, he says, see how it feels from the inside.

I think it will be the same, but I close my eyes and take a deep breath and feel for a minute. It turns out not to be scary.

His smell permeates the Indian cloth. It makes me feel like I am wearing his hair, his face, his sleep. It gives me a feeling of belonging.

My mother used to say: You've got a fine body. Use it. That's what it means to be a woman.

The day I started menstruating, she told me to take off my clothes. Now stand here, she said, and she walked me to the mirror on her closet door. Look at yourself. This is all any girl's got.

My body was still coated with baby fat; it made a belt around my waist, a ring around my cheeks. You have to start taking care of yourself, she said. You're a beautiful girl, but watch that fat. Boys want their girls skinny.

She'd told me ever since I could remember that I was born with it all: perfect face, perfect eyes, perfect hair. Use it right, like I do, she said. Don't blimp out; you'll end up as lonely as other girls. You'll have nothing. Go on a diet and you'll have it made.

Later that afternoon, I told her, Don't bring home so much stuff from your boyfriends anymore. I'm just eating once a day from now on.

In a few months, I leaned down to almost nothing. I stopped menstruating heavily. That was two years ago; I've bled lightly, and only once or twice, ever since. I guess that's why I don't get pregnant.

Thanks to my mother, I can get men to take care of me, drive fifty miles out of their way to drop me where I ask, share their bed with me for the night. My looks let me get anything I want.

Today he did not feel like working. He slept late, and first thing when he woke up poured himself the wine he hadn't finished last night. Now he wants to pick up more. He drinks too much, but I'm not going to say that. Finish what you've got slowly, I tell him. Let's get some painting done first.

It is the practice session for the second show. He is working on colonies of corals and long-stemmed sea plants. This was my idea; when I took off my clothes today, he couldn't decide which of his drawings to work on. I picked up his sketch pad and flipped through. Do the corals and the crinoids, I told him. He glanced at me for a second, and I wondered if I'd pronounced them correctly. But then he spread the drop cloth without a word and we went to work.

Where did you get such white hair? he asks. It's whiter than paper.

Genes, I say. But that's not true; I got it from a box. It's still down to my waist, but white, so no one can recognize me now. But he doesn't know that and he never will.

He sips wine from a jelly jar. And your lips — they're what fashion writers call petulant — do your parents have them too?

My mother does. Not my father. She told me his are as thin as pencil marks.

You don't see him?

He hasn't been around since I was a baby. But there've always been guys. She has lots of boyfriends.

I've got an ex-wife, he says, trailing the brush across the divide between the cheeks of my ass.

You got bored with her?

No, she kicked me out. She says I've got to get my act together before she'll even talk to me again.

You want her back?

I don't know. He places his hand on my hipbone, turns me so I'm angled away. You know, he says, some people accuse me of not finishing things. My marriage, my films, my whole goddamn career.

What's wrong with you? I want to ask. You have talent, after all. You have ideas, you have *me*. I glance at the jelly jar, and I hold myself back. I must play these cards right.

He glances up then. Any chance you'll get disenchanted with modeling before the seven weeks and move back with your mother?

No, I say. This is one thing you'll finish.

He nods, his eyes wet and big. He lowers his gaze to my hip.

Before I turned up he did a little of everything. Performance art, film. He came close to finishing the clothing movie but never edited the final print. Why don't you edit it now? I asked. Oh, he said, it's been so long, I couldn't concentrate on it anymore.

What he did finish were paintings of action, where he tried to present people in motion. Their arms and faces are blurs. We think we're here forever, he said, but life is so transitory. I asked what that meant, and he pulled out his dictionary and read the definition to me. That's how I learned how to look words up. But I don't feel right doing it in front of him. He might think it's weird.

When I first came to this city, my hair newly white, my shoulder bag dusty from the cabs of trucks where I'd slept, I found one of his ads on a bulletin board at the university. Artist model wanted, it said. That I can do at least as well as anyone else, I thought. I walked to his house; it was far out on the edge of the city, across the street from a junkyard. I waited on his steps as the air grew crisp and the reflections of sun on the mangled fenders softened into darkness. It was night by the time he showed up, but in the light from the junkyard I could see his face: cute as a boy, with eyes as deep as an old man's. My mother once told me, You can see everything in their eyes — if they can love, if they have disease. His eyes were special, a mix of sweet and sad, and somehow I knew before he said a word that he was a man I would wait for. I'm a model, I said. Let me come in and show you how I look.

Inside, he poured himself some wine, then studied me. I was wearing a pink dress, one of my mother's I'd taken

94

from her closet. You look so young, he said. I'm not sure I'd feel comfortable painting you nude.

Oh, I lied, in my family everyone looks young. I could vote this year, if there happened to be an election.

He said, Balthus couldn't ask for more. Only, I'll be honest with you — I don't have much money, so this isn't a full-time job.

That's OK. My mother pays the rent on my apartment, I said. More lies.

He sipped his wine and told me what he paid an hour. And I'll feed you when you're here, he added.

I asked him if he thought he'd ever make a name for himself. A few galleries like my work, he said, but in the art world you have to promote yourself. I guess sometimes I lose my drive, can't finish or don't push what I do.

I've got loads of drive, I said. Maybe some can wash off onto you. He smiled and raised his glass to his lips.

I found out about other projects, the few he'd finished, the many he hadn't. I asked him about them until cars stopped passing on the street and the room broke apart into shadows. It's late, he said. I'd hate to have you waiting for the trolley now. You can stay on the couch if you want. I took off my clothes as he stood there, stripped down to nothing and lowered myself onto his sofa. He turned and climbed the stairs to his studio, where his bed was, and shut off the hall light. I waited till I heard his mattress sigh, then went upstairs and lay down beside him, fitting my legs between his. You don't have to do that, he said, sliding away. I like you, and you can stay here tonight. But that's not necessary.

Right from the start, even before the show, he painted me constantly. He thought I was an experienced model; I could hold poses with barely a twitch. It was his fatigue, the cramps in his body, that made us stop at night. Then he would suggest I sleep over. Nothing funny, he'd say. But it's too late for you to go home.

Most nights went like this. Those that didn't, when instead of painting he met with gallery owners or rich people or friends at a bar downtown, I found other places to sleep. That meant, always, looking into eyes and saying words I didn't believe, letting my hair be touched, my breasts cupped, my thighs parted by the hands of a face I would never see again. I am lucky this way: the genes that made me up were a perfect mix. The bones go just so far, and no farther — right to where they should be. I should have nothing to fear; I should do well in life.

We are watching TV. The news is on. I never watched it before, but he likes to at night.

I look down. My knees poke out from the opening of his bathrobe. Even though I have just showered, I can see all the paintings that have led up to today layered under my skin. He tells me my flesh is recording time, like the earth.

The Cambrian period, he says, pointing to the remnants of the amoebas during a commercial.

The Silurian, I add, outlining the coral from today.

He blinks. You've been reading my books? he says, glancing toward the corner, where the entire *Life Nature Library* is heaped. Each book is open; the glossy pictures of prehistoric creatures, fertilized eggs, transparent fish, have lain on the floor for weeks. I didn't know you liked to read, he says.

I don't, I say, though it's hard to know; books were not something I ever had at home. Just because I look at pictures, I say, doesn't mean I like to read.

He nods. His bottle of wine is empty. I can find stronger soap, if you want, he says.

I don't mind, I tell him. I smile and let the robe fall open. He smiles back at me, then turns and faces the television.

Three days till the second show, and the review of the first comes out in the paper. There is one review for the whole show, but our piece, me, is the subject of two small articles to itself.

One is a regular review. It says we are innovative, that my painted body evokes the beauty of a primeval sea. The writer compares me to Gaia, a mother-goddess, a life source. "Some would call it a throwback to the body painting of the '60s, but this is different," he writes. "This body penetrates to our collective unconscious, and with its careful strokes and evolving story it is far from the stagnant though pretty wallpaper that was painted on women's bodies years ago."

The other is an article about the reactions of groups at the university. Some claim we are indecent; others claim we are exploiters. "Women have stopped defining themselves strictly by their bodies," one is quoted as saying. "This show suggests that such a change never occurred; that women are and will forever be objects. What we have here is a public celebration of misogyny." Another group says, "Art can encompass many things, but live nudity belongs in the domain of the pornographer, not the artist. We are appalled that this university is funding such a flagrant display of decadence. Parents who care about morality would do well to think twice before writing that next tuition check."

He snaps the newspaper closed. Censorship, he says. They tried it with that guy who used body fluids. They'll try it with anyone who challenges their run-of-the-mill conceptions. Fascists.

I glance toward the dictionary. This is all getting so involved I suddenly feel over my head, but from the tone of his voice I figure out what to say. It's a free country, I blurt out. If we want to say something, we can say it.

He sits back in his chair, staring at the table.

I go on, though I've never thought about this before: If I want to define myself by my body, that's fine. Because if we don't do what we want, we risk being forced into something else.

What do you mean? he says.

Like — I don't know. Like something we're not.

He peers at me. Do you really think this? he asks.

Yeah, I say. Sure.

But sitting here, watching his hair wave in the draft from the window, I realize they are just words I am saying, words he wants to hear. They sound right, but what do I care about this. What really matters is permanent warmth. Everything else is nothing.

People flock to the second show, some inside the gallery with glasses perched on their noses, others outside with placards raised high. On my legs, sponges cluster in colonies; they seem to be streaming down my body, toward my extended foot. Amoebas take refuge on this foot. A few are incomplete, their other halves having been chased off my toes into oblivion.

Most of the people focus on me.

Through the windows I can see handwritten signs. SLASH THE FUNDS: STOP THE PEEP SHOW, says one. Wait a minute, I want to say, isn't a lot of art about naked women? Then another sign comes into view: IN HERE ALL WOMEN ARE OBJECTS. But I am not all women, and I am not an object. Besides, who are they to tell me what to do with my body? On the opposite side of the building are more signs. One reads, A WOMAN'S BODY IS HER CASTLE. I prefer that, though in a way it is as offensive as the others. I am only one woman. My body does not stand for anything. It is mine. That is all. It is mine — and it is his.

I think, as I stand, about him, about us, about how he does not know I am lying to him. I think about those first lies, and the ones that followed; how quickly they slid from my lips, as easy as a kiss. But he's never doubted what I've said. He needs me too much.

And then I think about the morning after a gallery had decided against taking the action pictures he'd painted of me. He had pinned all his hopes on getting in there, and the next day when I came by, he was still in bed. I thought you wanted to work today, I'd said. I can't do it anymore, he'd replied, and he rolled over and faced the wall.

I sat by his pillow for a minute. After a while I said, Let's do something different today.

It'll all be the same. It'll never change.

Maybe not, but we can still have fun. Look, why don't you try painting something new.

Like what.

Like, and I'd looked out his window to the junkyard, like hubcaps or bottles or car roofs.

He didn't say anything.

Or an animal. Paint some animal. A dog. Me.

It's been done, he said.

Then do it new. Do it your way.

I don't know what that is anymore.

Come on, I'll help you figure it out. I'd taken hold of his arm and pulled until he sat up.

And you know that Works in Progress show at the university that you wanted to enter? With such good money in it? Enter me.

He shook his head and laughed. That's a long shot.

Maybe, I said. Maybe not.

★

We have three weeks to go. Every morning, we read the newspaper to each other. He reads me the news. I read him the editorials. I am getting better at understanding what they're about, and asking him to define the words he uses: Machiavellian, seditious, parasitic. I will not look them up in front of him, but when I ask him questions, he seems to feel so good. And sometimes, just to show he's had an effect on me, I use the words later, if they seem to apply to the paintings. Like these fish and the seaweed — that's symbiotic, right?

He starts, stares at my leg. I guess so, he says. You know, I think you're smarter than you give yourself credit for.

I tell him to keep painting.

Every few days, there are letters to the editor about the show at the university, and inevitably, they focus on me. There are so many arguments, I can't keep track of them all. "Now you see what happens when we fund any Joe Quasi-Artist off the street. Money should not be squandered on immorality," one letter says. Another, anonymous, is so short, I almost miss it. In its entirety it reads: "And they wonder why they get raped?"

I know it is not hopeless if I work things right. I did it once before, when I lived in that other city.

A boy, that first one in the alley, became my brother. His father moved in with my mother and brought him along. That first night, we eyed each other across the living room, waited till we heard the springs creak in my mother's bed, then stole into my room. Below us the boys were getting high in the alley. We closed the window. I'd never felt a sheet beneath me when I did it. It made me feel like an angel.

We hung out every night. The other boys didn't like it. You're ours, they'd say. We'll take you back soon enough, soon as he bags you. Don't worry, he'd tell me. You're my woman. I'll take care of you.

And he did. He was strong, with a body so big that when he stood in a doorway, he could block almost all the light; when he lay over me, and came down low on his elbows, he would cover me completely — he became my ceiling and sky. Other boys never dared go after me with him around. He walked by my side always, his arm around my shoulders.

Then one of his old girlfriends called him up and said she was going to have his baby. But I haven't seen you for months, he said. Sorry, she said, four more weeks and I'm popping. You want to see it, you come by.

I got to go, he told me, packing. I can't do nothing.

Think you'll stay with her? I asked, throwing some things in a shoulder bag, thinking stupidly that maybe I could go along.

Till the kid's born, he said. After that, I don't know.

Next morning I told my mother I was walking him to the bus.

He's a good kid, his father said. My mother put her arm around her man. What did she know. I hiked my bag up higher on my shoulder and cursed this old girlfriend. If only I could have gotten pregnant first. But then I'd have to share him.

The other boys ground broken glass under their sneakers as they watched my brother and me walk down the block. They said nothing. He held my hand.

At the end of the street I turned and looked at them. They shot kisses up the sidewalk at me. My brother jerked my hand. I turned my back on them. All the way to the bus, I could feel them staring. They would be waiting for me to return. They would gun me down on the street with their eyes.

★

The sixth show is packed. Around me, canvases are filling up, marble is smoothing down into figures. Dinosaurs are dying across my body. The protesters are still outside. They will argue their case before the finance committee tomorrow, but we are planning that Homo sapiens will cover me next week.

The show is almost over, and I am looking forward to going home, when a large man with skin the color of gray stone comes in. I am twisting at the waist, my arms reaching toward the ceiling so the pterodactyls appear to be flying. The man heads right for my side. He winds through the crowd, brushing people out of his way like weeds. They sway back, unaware, it seems, of his touch. There is something familiar about him, not his face but the way he moves, the way his eyes are lit. He reminds me of the boys.

I am standing there, posing as though I am trying to climb into Heaven, when this man walks up. His head is even with mine, despite the pedestal. I glance away and find my artist. He is talking to someone. He is in the middle of saying something and he freezes, his hands caught spread and speaking, and he turns his head toward me. I peer back at the man. My eyes are looking right into his. He is staring at me.

And then he grabs me and jerks me down from the pedestal and presses me into him and clamps his mouth onto mine. I try to scream, but my voice cannot get out. His breath tastes of onions and beer, the wool of his coat scratches my skin like a brick wall, I try to push away but he's too strong, I can't wriggle out of his grip. All around, I hear the cries of people, the artists — my artist — the security guards, the stomping of feet. Clear the way! Doors are slammed shut. His tongue twists into me. I can feel his rough hands kneading into my waist, kneading the paint right off my skin.

All right, buddy, they shout. Dozens of fingers squeeze between us and try to pry him off me. The skin of one hand is covered with bumps — the raised paint of my artist. He is here. He'll do something. He will —

But the stone man won't let go. I'm squirming, I'm kicking, the hands are like crowbars, I'm wrenching my head this way and that, there are bodies all around me, men everywhere: Let her go! they yell.

I open my eyes. He is looking right at me. His eyes are as gray as the stone of his skin. The lines in them run wild, like someone carved up the whites with a razor.

And then I feel air on my skin, he is breaking away from me; they've got him now. His mouth drops off mine, but his eyes are locked onto me, and as the police wrest him away, he leans toward me and rasps: Baby, baby, you are a gift from God.

Once he is off me, he holds out his hands, and the police slap on the cuffs. I cough and gasp for air. He grins at me until they turn him around and lead him out.

It is then that I see the gallery has been cleared. Outside, voices are shouting so many things I cannot hear any of them. Security guards linger at the door.

You all right? my artist says, and he lays his hand on my back. I lower my head, cover my eyes with my fingers, breathe. I thought you were going to get him off me, I say. I thought you were going to take care of me.

He was a big guy. Strong. Think I broke some fingers.

He holds up his right hand, his painting hand. The three long fingers are swollen, bent sideways and backward, and covered with blood. Looks like this counts us out for the finish, he says.

I am changing the dressing on his fingers. The seventh show is tonight, but we will not be there; we had to withdraw.

The finance committee, seeing no reason to pursue, canceled the hearing. It will be several weeks before my artist can paint again. I'd tried to relax in what would have been our last week together, but instead I worried about my future with him. So I have been cooking his meals. I have been scrubbing the paint off his bathtub.

You know, you don't need to stay here, he says when I finish wrapping the bandage.

But I want to. I want to keep you up and busy.

I can't be busy if I can't work.

Sure you can. Let's go somewhere. Let's do something.

What.

Anything to get out of your studio. It's still light out; how about if we go sit on your front steps and watch the sun set over the junkyard?

He brings a jug of wine. I sip some water. Trolleys and cars pass by, men in overalls stroll home from work. A fine mist has settled onto the street; there are no colors in the sky.

I know I cannot wait any longer.

I take his hurt hand and press it between my two. He does not resist. His skin is rough and hard, as coarse as the bandage that surrounds his fingers. Do you like me? I ask him, placing his hand beneath my skirt, squeezing it between my thighs.

He turns to me and smiles. Yes, he says, and he outlines my cheekbones with a finger from his other hand. You've been what I needed. I'll always like you.

Will you stay with me? I ask.

I feel his hand go limp. I'm not the person you want, he says. I can't even take care of myself.

But we're a team. Look at the publicity we got.

Nothing lasts long in the art world. Something new will come up, and people will forget about us.

I want to make us last, I say.

He smiles quietly into the distance.

And then he bends over and kisses me, for the first time, on my lips. Our mouths are closed, our lips puckered like little hearts. This is what I'd wanted for so long, this is what I'd worked for. But as he pulls away, I realize: there was no passion in his kiss. Nothing I've done has worked; he did not touch me as a lover. I cannot believe it. I swallow to stop shaking inside.

You are not like a father, I say, stroking his face.

You are too much like a daughter, he replies, removing my hand.

He folds my arms in my lap and turns. I follow his gaze, but there is nothing I want to see.

I could sit here until I found a man walking by who appealed to me. Then I could stop him with a toss of my hair. Or I could leave right now, go downtown, find a man on a corner licking his lips, sweating, burning to guide my fingers toward his belt. I could do whatever I want, but as I sit on these steps watching possibilities stroll by, I decide to stay here, just one more night. Tomorrow I'll say good-bye and walk to a store, and there I'll put on a little eye shadow, a little lipstick and blush. I'll check myself in a mirror. I'll decide how I'm going to look.

I peer down at my legs. Below the stockings, I spy the outline of the paintings, frozen in motion. Then I look harder, and I realize that I am seeing nothing but the chilly rising of my own veins. The paint has washed away. All that is left is me.

THE LONG SADNESS
OF NO

WHEN MY MOTHER turned seventeen, she fell in love with a man who had multiple sclerosis. For dates, she and Peter rode buses, looping through one town after another in the slanting sunlight of each afternoon. They sat close, the sides of their bodies touching, their hair weaving into the wool of each other's sweaters. He whispered funny stories about other passengers; she giggled. They rode until night fell, and on that final run they would slouch down and kiss, stopping only when my mother noticed that they had passed Peter's stop. Then he reached for his cane, and shuffled off the bus, and poked through the brown leaves shriveling on the sidewalks. She inched along, holding on to steady him. The few blocks to his house often took an hour. Afterward, she ran home, keeping in the street, as far as she could get from shadows and strangers.

If my mother was awake during the afternoon naps we took together before I was old enough for school, I would ask her about Peter. She told me about the stars he notched into his cane after their trips, about the melted-chocolate sound of his voice. She never refused to answer my questions. And I asked so many. Sometimes, when she and I were riding in the car, or cooking dinner, and there was a lull in our conversation, I would pick up where we'd left off the day or the week before. On occasion, her stories about him made her voice crack, and she would turn and hug me. I always squeezed hard when I hugged back.

Once, when the whole family was at the shore, and my father was hauling the beach chairs back to the car, and my mother was holding the baby, and the rest of us were grumbling about the hot sand, I ran up to her and asked why she hadn't married Peter. She did not say, "I fell out of love with him." Nor did she say, "He fell out of love with me."

She said, "Because then I'd have to do everything by myself. Like carry those beach chairs and your sister at the same time."

I tried to protest but I didn't know what to say. It simply made too much sense.

Later, after the divorce, when my brothers and sisters and I pleaded with my mother to explain why she ever married my father in the first place, she told us, "I was so depressed after I broke up with Peter that I couldn't see straight. I used to walk in front of cars. . . . Then someone introduced me to your father . . ."

Now she is almost sixty, and has gone through two more marriages and countless other men. Sometimes she goes to singles dances. Inevitably she ends up in the ladies room, weeping behind a stall door so she doesn't have to face anyone, not even herself in the mirror. She calls me from a nearby pay phone, where she twists the segmented cord around her fingers like a spiral of rings, occasionally pulling so hard she breaks the connection and has to call back. I come and drive her home. She begs me to spend the night on her sofa. I cannot say no.

Last night I had a dream about Peter. In it, I find him in an institution, sitting in a wheelchair. I come up to him and tell him who my mother is. His eyes widen as he takes me in — I have my mother's body, I have her skin and her lips. His face grows flushed, and in that melted-chocolate voice I've imagined so many times, he asks, "Can I see her? Can I see her?" I run to a phone across the room, call and tell her that I have found him. "It's a miracle," I say. "He is waiting for you to drive over." "After all these years?" she says. "I can't. I feel too guilty." She hangs up. I stare at the wall while I gather the courage to explain this, and then I turn around, but even across the room he has heard everything; already he is crumpled and sobbing in his wheelchair. When I wake up, I am crying too, and my body is stiff with the paralysis that comes from sleeping in the wrong position.

I will not tell my mother about my dream. It would only be cruel. Life is hard enough without your children tugging at your sleeve, bringing up things that cannot be changed.

GRANDMA DEATH

I FOUND THE FIRST ONE on my way to work. It was in the bathroom at the bus terminal.

I'd just come out of the toilet and was slinging my purse over my shoulder when I happened to notice, under the stall door right in front of me, a dark hand with blue-gray nails and fingers curled in like a claw. I looked harder and could make out the arm behind it, soaking up a puddle of water. I bent down and peeked inside the stall. That was when I saw the head, resting against the base of the john. The legs must've been back there somewhere, but I sure wasn't about to look for them.

I ran to the sinks, didn't see anyone, so I went out to the ticket booth and told the man behind the counter. I wanted to stay for the big scene — ambulance, doctor, body bag — but I had to get to work. George, my boss, says I'm lucky to have a job at Shop-Rite, they usually don't hire old women like me because we work too slow and suffer from arthritis and eye trouble. I myself don't work too slow, and all he can say about me is I'm stout and short. But my friends from high school, those that're still alive, are half blind and humpbacked and move like molasses. They would've had a stroke just walking into the bathroom at the bus station, let alone finding someone on the floor. So I know what he means.

Next morning I saw it in the *Daily News*: Drug Death in Philadelphia Bus Station. I've read the paper every day of my life, but this was the first time I saw my own name in it. I cut the article out and at work taped it to my cash register. Freddie the stock boy said I was brave, especially for an old lady. I said, Bravery had nothing to do with it, and stop calling me an old lady. He said, Sorry, and just before closing he took the shoppers' music off the loud-speakers and rapped a little song about it. Lazy kid. Should be working, not wasting his time.

That night I called my son Jacob. He's the best of all my kids. Can talk about current events without getting too far from what I think or pushing any cockamamie ideas. Comes over to play pinochle when I ask him to and otherwise leaves me alone. Not like the others. They're always calling up, You all right, Ma? We're worried about you. I can predict every word they say — anything too deep for Erma Bom-beck, they don't even think about. Never visit when I want them and always bothering me when I don't. Jacob's wife is pregnant. My sixth grandchild but first from her. Finally. He said, Be careful, Ma. We don't want anything to happen to you. That bus station's in a bad part of town, you know. I said, Don't get all worked up. I'm no junkie like that bimbo was.

I thought that was it. But two weeks later I found the second one.

I'd gone out back and was dragging the trash cans down the alley to the street when I saw this big green Hefty bag lying crossways in front of me, just below the living room window on the side of the house. One end of the bag looked like a cantaloupe, the other like a big carrot, and in between like a sack of potatoes. I went to kick it out of the

116

way and my foot hit something soft. I decided it wasn't potatoes.

So I put down the trash and ran inside and called the cops. This time I didn't have to go to work so I was able to wait around. Two cops came, two know-it-alls who thought I was making a big deal over a sack of litter till they untied the bag and we all got a look. That's Nicki Lazaro, I told them — he'd never shown up for some big trial, who wouldn't know his face. Damn if it isn't, they said. They shook my hand and radioed for help.

Two cars came, then three, then four. Soon the whole sidewalk was full of them, talking and taking fingerprints and shooing away reporters. My neighbor Nadine came home and had to get escorted to her door. She looked like she was going to cry. Me, I never shed tears, not even when my husband died. He kept a bottle of schnapps in the glove compartment, drank to and from work, and at home whiskey in the basement. I learned early, there's nothing to be gained by crying.

The next day George himself taped the new clipping onto my cash register. I was right up there on page one, side by side with heads of states. A lot of the shoppers recognized me from the picture, and half a dozen stuck around to ask questions, making my line get all backed up. I didn't want to be bothered, but what can you do. Everyone wanted to hear about it. They treated me so special, it was like I'd been the one that died and I'd come back to tell them about it.

That night Donna, my youngest daughter, called. She's always whining about something that's not right, her job, her house, whatever. She'd been planning her wedding, all the time yakking about pleasing everyone — Politics, she informed me, must be handled with subtlety, feelings are as delicate as doilies, Mother, I'm sure this is something

those diplomats you read about know all too well — until
I told her I didn't want to have anything to do with it. I
couldn't stand to spend seven months of her juggling the
bridesmaids, the seating arrangements, the colors of the
clothes, everything. Why doesn't she just elope. That'd
spare us all.

Donna acted all upset. Ma, what're you doing living in
a place where the Mafia dumps bodies, she said. I said, Just
one body, and look, I've lived here since you were a baby
and I'm not going to leave now. Besides, it's close to work.
She said, Arthur says you can come stay with us when we
get married. I said, Nothing doing. I can live how I want
here.

Donna made sure everyone else called me, but I held my
ground. Dead bodies can pop up anywhere. There's a lot
of us living, so there'll be a lot of us dying. That's just the
way it is.

A few days later, I gazed out the window at work and in
the street beyond the parking lot a teenager who was being
chased by a woman in curlers ran in front of a car and got
blown clear across the roof of the A&P. The next night,
while I was out buying a present for the new baby, I glanced
at the guy in front of me. One minute he was tapping the
sales counter with his credit card, the next he was sprawled
on the floor, hands clutching his chest. That weekend I was
walking down the street to buy a can of soda. Two sisters
in separate cars slammed head-on into each other. While
riding the Monday bus home from work, I looked out the
window. The Aliens and the Boostmen broke their truce
and stormed onto enemy corners, slicing one another into
coleslaw. Even strolling in the park a week later, I saw a
retired gym teacher skid on his bicycle, sail over his han-
dlebars, and smash into a brick wall.

Every time, I was quick to find a phone and call the police. They'd come and pat me on the back and say, Good work, Bea. They got to know me. They started calling me their divining rod. You got a nose for death, they'd say. You're better than Jeane Dixon.

Freddie thought it was great and began keeping a Bea Glatt bulletin board in the front of the store. He called me Grandma Death. People would come behind the belt so their relatives could snap a picture of them alongside me. George said we were beating out the A&P across the street for the first time in years.

My kids phoned all the time until one night I yelled at them to stop. All this attention, it was really starting to get to me.

The next day my children showed up at my house. All five of them plus spouses, and the grandchildren too. The girls wore party dresses, the boys suits, and the women new curls and flowers in their hair, even Donna, who usually lets the weather do her styling. The first thing I said was, What're you doing coming here dressed like refugees from a wedding. There's no party. I got things to do. They said, We just wanted to visit you, Ma. You're precious to us. See? We brought you a cake and some presents.

So everyone sat around the kitchen table and ate the cake. I cleared my throat and did some laundry and showed my general irritation. I told them to wash their own dishes and while they did I sat in the living room, nose in the paper. When everything was clean and put away, they packed themselves around me and pulled out presents. One of the grandkids gave me a silver star made out of tin foil which he pinned on me so I'd be the official sheriff. Another handed me sea monkeys. They never die, Grandma, she said. You just add water when they stop moving.

I said, You're trying to make me feel bad for finding all these dead people. Well, I'll have you know I have nothing whatsoever to do with it. They just appear and I report them.

We're not trying to make you feel bad, they said. That's the furthest thing from our minds.

They took a roll of pictures — the first time in maybe three years anyone but Jacob thought to bring a camera — and Donna's fiancé made a videotape of the kids kissing me. I told them I had to take a nap. From my front window I watched them get into their cars. I wondered if any of them would die soon. Not that I wanted them to, especially not Jacob. I just wondered.

A month and eight corpses later, I got a wake-up call from a producer in Hollywood who asked to make a movie of me. He just called out of the blue. A story of your life, Mrs. Glatt, he said. At first I thought it was a joke, but he wired me a contract the same day. I stared at the letter in the Western Union office. With this money, I could pay off the mortgage and my debts and even panel the living room in gold if I wanted. Finally I'd have the good life. I signed the contract right there in Western Union and sent it back. On my way out, a truck on the street lost control and plowed into an office building. I didn't wait around to see what happened.

That night, all these reporters came by with their cameras running and mikes growing out of their hands. We hear from our sources in Hollywood you got a movie contract, they said. You'll put Philadelphia on the map. They asked if I'd ever seen anyone die before the junkie in the bathroom. No, I said. Not even when I miscarried twenty-eight years ago.. Not even when my husband died.

Then one of them laughed nervously and said, So tell us,

you've seen so much death — do you have a way of knowing ahead of time who's going to die?

I said, Hey, I'm not the Grim Reaper, if that's what you
mean. I just see what's already there.

He said, Well, there's a lot of people out there who think
you have magic powers, that you're making this happen.

That's crazy, I said.

The next day at work, shoppers peered inside the plate glass
and when they saw me, spun around and headed to the
A&P. The place was so empty that I had time to browse
through a tabloid at my register. The lead article was about
me, my face covering the front page and under it the caption,
Grandma Death. I glanced up to mention this to the other
cashiers, but they'd all called in sick, so I read the two pages,
then turned to the crossword puzzle. Halfway through my
shift, George tiptoed over, head down, and said, I'm asking
you nice. Please go home for the day. I said, Paid? He said,
Anything you want.

So I went home and settled down to some soap operas
and potato chips and waited for Donna or Jacob or any
of the others to call and congratulate me for making it
into the movies. The soap operas turned into the evening
shows. I ate a bowl of soup, watched more TV, and still
they didn't call. I'd raised them to read the paper every day.
I used to tell them, The world is bigger than your own
backyard, and knowing how things work is the only way
to feel you've got any control at all. But here they were,
ignorant of my fame. Well, it wasn't going to be me that
told them. I waited up all night for someone else to do the
enlightening.

In the morning the phone rang. It was George. He said,
We're going to have to let you go. We'll send you a check
for the next ten years.

Fine, I said. Who needs Shop-Rite anyway, when Holly-wood's waiting.

I brought the phone into my front hallway, where I could hear it when my kids got wind of the big news, and I sat on my steps in the sun to catch Nadine the minute she came home so I could crow to her about the movie. All day long, not a single car passed on the street. Not a single person, either. The block was quiet, and when it got dark Nadine's windows were still black. At eleven-thirty I went inside.

Three days I waited, first on my steps, then in my living room. Finally I called Donna, just to see if she had any idea what was going on in the world at all. Her phone rang twice but when a voice came on it wasn't her, it was a recording saying the line had been disconnected, and there was no forwarding number available. One by one I tried the others and with each I heard a recording and that's how I started to get the picture. I saved Jacob for last, but even with him it was the same.

So I called the only person I thought would care. The Hollywood producer.

Hello? I said, Is this the office of Mr. So-and-So?

Yes, it is, a woman said, but he's not here anymore.

Don't tell me he moved too, I said. Everyone's taking off on me.

He didn't move, she said. He had a coronary. Yesterday. Haven't you heard?

I threw down the phone. If I didn't figure something out, I'd spend the rest of my life stuck in that house with nothing to do, seeing car accidents and CLOSED signs whenever I went out.

For days I sat on the sofa, not doing anything. Sunlight would come in the east window, creep across the rug, and slip out the west window. Water dripped from the kitchen sink. I waited for the mailman, but he never came. Waited for the gas reader — once a month would be enough for me, but he didn't come when he was supposed to either. I listened to what the city sounds like when there are no voices. Except for the clunks of the corner traffic light as it changed green to yellow to red, I didn't hear a thing, not birds, not even insects. No oil truck filling my tank, no young couple fighting next door. The quiet was so loud it hurt my ears.

After a few weeks I figured I had to do *something*. I tried dealing myself up for solitaire but got nothing but face cards, nines, and tens, and then I remembered Jacob's pinochle deck was all I had in the house. So I turned on the TV — reruns only, just to be safe — only every person reminded me of someone I'd known, and later that afternoon the picture blinked out because the electricity stopped running. And when I picked up the phone to call a repairman, I found my line was dead. That night, in the dark and the quiet, I puzzled it out: I hadn't got mail so I hadn't paid my bills. Soon everything stopped working except the water.

It's been maybe six weeks. I stopped going upstairs or showering; now I live on the sofa. My food's almost gone so I make half a can of soup last a day, and with the heat out I'm always huddled under a blanket. I want more than anything to go to a sale in a department store or get stuck on a rush hour bus or even haggle with Donna over the cut of her wedding dress. But everyone thinks I can cause deaths, and it's reached the point where I'm not sure if I can or I can't.

On the sofa, under the blanket, I keep busy by thinking about Jacob. I wouldn't risk getting in touch, and besides, I have no idea where he is, so I've taken to writing him letters in my head. Stop by for a round, I tell him. Bring your deck, we'll mix it with mine. We'll take our sweet time playing.

By now I've written about fifty letters. I don't sleep much anymore, my mind's so busy scribbling.

Jacob, I say, I've been wondering if you're thinking about me. I want to hear what you would have to say about my life. I wish I could even imagine your reply.

MAGNET HILL

YOU NEED A WAY OUT when you date idiot guys. I mean something to shove between you, something to hold them off. Like doors, they're good. And streets, they're better. Busy streets. Fat, crowded, city ones. Me, look at me, I lost my worst date in Philly, took off when his eyes were turned. Slipped into this record store across the street, watched him through the window with cars shooting by, watched him look for me, his mouth hanging open like a door in summer. Got bored and bought some records, then checked out a bar on my fake ID, met a few guys, drank beer. Had a good time.

This is what I say to my girlfriend Jeannine. We're on our lunch break at Burger King, where we work. Jeannine, I tell her, guys are what I know best, you should listen. She says, You're right, but sometimes it isn't so easy for me. You're smart, you can think fast. I can't. I just end up going along for the ride.

Girl, you gotta use your head, I say, use your noggin, God gave it to you for some reason right?

Jeannine, she's a wimp, never knows what to do, and I tell you, I can't stand it, she goes along with everything. She's still in high school and hates it. Won't do the smart thing and leave. Her folks would throw her out if she did. No problem, I say to her, there's a room open down the hall from me. No, she says, I gotta stay, they'd hate me if I left. She doesn't need the money, but since her brother runs the Burger King her folks make her help.

While I'm talking, Jeannine's playing with this gold necklace that spells out her name in script. Fine, right, she says, but what if you're with a guy and you're not near home? This last guy, Bob? He took me to the mall, took me to this sick movie with blood, and I said I didn't like it but he wouldn't leave —

Hey, Philly's near Wilkes-Barre? I say. But I was smart, I brought money. You gotta take care of yourself.

Well, OK, what if someone asks you out when you don't have money on you but you like him and then it stinks. Then what do you do? Once I was hanging in the mall and the hottest guy came up and we started talking and he asked me to go for a ride so I went, but it wasn't what he wanted, a ride, I mean.

Well, you figure something out. Did you?

She shakes her head no, looks down at her fries.

You shoulda done like me. I do what I need to. The motto is, Don't let them win, never let them win. Like once I was down in Wildwood and I met this guy who drove me to his hotel to do some coke. He wouldn't stop talking, went on and on about his ex-girlfriend, his parents. A *real* bore. I said, I gotta go now, and he said, But it's been so long since I've had someone to talk to, and he laid out another line. Finally I went to the bathroom. At first I thought about the window, but it was the fourth floor, I couldn't do that. So I found his shaving cream, sprayed it on my hair till I looked like I was in a Prell commercial. I came out, said, coke makes me wild, I drank all your Listerine. You wanna take off your clothes? I got this thing about ripping off Band-Aids.

He drove me home fast, you'd better believe it.

Jeannine looks at me, sucks on a fry. She thinks over what I say. To her I'm like a big sister, like a teacher. I'm eighteen and tall and my tits are big and stand up without a bra, and guys can't help seeing me. I'm a neon sign on a back country road. Jeannine respects that, it's how she wants to be.

Jeannine's sixteen, dumpy, cute like a puppy. She's got good hair, and she highlights it too. Laughs a lot around guys, never knows what to say. Gives in even if it's not what she wants because she doesn't like to hurt them. It's crazy she's that way. I coach her. I say, Hey, don't worry, they're flies at a picnic. Swat them, and others'll buzz right in to take their place.

She listens to me. Not like the other girls here. They've got boyfriends, one each, some of them guys I dumped. These girls, they talk about me over the grill, call me a cold bitch, a ball breaker. Right before Jeannine came to work here in June, I almost told them off. But I felt the same way I did a few years ago, when I finally got wise and left my father's house — not that I didn't want to chew him out, but I figured, why the hell bother.

Jeannine, she likes me, calls me her best friend. I got her to stop playing rusky roulette, got her on the pill. Made her wear make-up, learn to dress tight, so guys look. I tell her, Remember: always be in control. *You're* the one who makes them look, *you're* the one who makes them get lost.

Sometimes I get angry with her, she's such a kid. Doesn't know what to do with herself. Sometimes she makes me think of people on TV, in places where they get these floods. You see pictures of them getting carried away by the water, reaching out their arms. . . . Sometimes they grab hold of a house or a tree and save themselves. But sometimes they get swept away with the brown water and broken-up cars. That's how I think about Jeannine. And it drives me nuts that anyone can be like that.

In August, a couple months after we got to be friends, these two guys start in on us. Right away, they come three times a day, order Pepsis. They pull their money out in balls from their pockets, it's all wrinkled. I like the tall one, Lion. His eyes are green, his hair's blond, and it's got a good, strong wave that carries it like a thick rope down the back of his neck. When he gives me his money, he slides his fingers slowly over my palm like it's cat fur. I look at him, smile, let out air through my mouth. He nods once, quick.

The other guy, Johnny, is scrawny-looking, but Jeannine tells me she likes him. I don't know why, all he does is laugh and his hair falls in his face. One of his eyes keeps drifting off to the side like it keeps remembering it's got somewhere else to go. But who knows about these things.

They start asking us stuff like how old we are and where we live. The taller one does the asking. Jeannine blushes, puts their Pepsis on the tray. The smaller one watches. She looks up at him every few seconds, bites her lip. I answer questions for us both.

Then today before her shift, her brother — the manager — comes up to me. I been watching you, he says. Be careful what you do with my sister, she's real young. Hell, you were born older than she is now. I won't say you can't hang out together, but keep an eye on her, OK? I don't want nothing bad happening.

Yeah, I say. I can't believe she puts up with this crap, but I don't tell him that.

He must've seen it coming, because at dinner the guys ask us what we're doing after work. I feel Jeannine look at me. Nothing, I say, and glance at her. She nods, eyes wide. The big one says, So let's go for a ride, what do you think? Sure, I say, great, fine.

Her brother sees them waiting in the parking lot at closing. When Jeannine's in the kitchen, he says to me, Remember what I said.

Don't worry, I say, Control is my specialty, it's where I get straight A's.

In the ladies room, we change to miniskirts and sandals. She curls her hair, I mousse mine, and we go out. It's still hot and sticky, the kind of weather that makes you want to pull your skin off and fan it back and forth so you can cool down.

Lion shows us their car, a '71 Chevy. The hubcaps are smeared with mud, the bumper sticker reads: ROCK 'N' ROLL ANIMALS. I get in front because Lion's driving.

The radio blasts out soon as he turns the key. I look at him from the side. This way I can see his cheek, between his ear and his lips, where it makes a smooth valley. I want to reach over and skate my fingers down that valley, down his neck.

But I don't. I gotta watch out for Jeannine.

We turn off the highway when we hit the end of the strip and head out to farmland. I don't know this area. I say, You guys live here? Naw, Lion says, we live over in Trucksville, we just like cruising around. We found this place we want to take you to. Ever hear of Magnet Hill?

No, I say.

That's 'cause we just named it, he says. Right, Johnny?

M-m-m-m-m-agnet Hill, yeah, Johnny stutters from the back. He beats out the drum parts to the song on the radio, fast, it sounds like he's running. I glance over my shoulder. Him and Jeannine are sitting close, not looking at each other.

You brothers? I ask Lion.

Yeah, he says, think I'd hang out with him if we wasn't? He laughs, and so does Johnny. Johnny sucks in when he laughs, like the Burger King door when it closes too fast.

We drive down roads I've never been on, up and down hills, into woods, past fields and barns. Everything twists around. I lose track of direction, I keep waiting to hit the Susquehanna or the mountains so I can figure it out.

The radio's up real loud and they pass around a joint. Lion and me say lots of stupid things. I ask about his name, and he says it's because of his hair and also he's not afraid to do anything, anything at all. He winks at me. Then he faces the road again and says, Why d'ya think Johnny's called Johnny?

I don't know, I say, Scotch, right? He doesn't answer, they both just laugh. Jeannine squeaks out a tiny giggle, I can't tell what she thinks is funny, maybe it's just the pot.

Finally we come to this place between two hills. The land scoops in like it's a hammock with a fat man in the middle. At the tops of the hills are trees, but where we are, in the center, it's just grass or weeds. With the moon on so bright, it looks like frost. The sky around the moon is dark, I can see a million stars, and the roach has gone out in my hand.

This here's Magnet Hill. Lion turns off the car.

We sit there. The crickets sing away. I wait for Lion's hand to sneak up my leg or for Johnny to make some crack.

But no one does anything. We sit and wait. And when it happens, it's not what I ever thought.

What happens is the car starts rolling up the hill — *backwards*. The motor's not even on and it's moving. It's like something's sucking it up, slowly, like we're in a straw. We didn't start it, we can't stop it, we just gotta go along.

Jeannine says the first thing she's said since we got in the car. She says, What's going on? She sounds real scared.

Lion holds his hands up to show her they're not on the steering wheel. See, he says, Magnet Hill. Next to her, Johnny laughs. The car moves faster and faster up the hill, like whatever's sucking us is getting stronger and stronger. It makes Johnny laugh more.

Then Jeannine starts saying, I don't like this. When does it stop? There could be another car over the hill. Why is this happening?

It's OK, Lion says, no one else hangs out here.

I don't like it, I don't like it, she says. I think, Yeah, I don't like this either. Only I'm not going to say it.

Air blows through the window, strong, then weak, then strong again. It feels like it's kicking my face.

We gotta pull over, I say, Jeannine'll flip. Lion gives me this look, I rub my hand over his knee and inside near his thigh and he hits the brakes.

The car jerks fast and we stop. I feel like we're still moving, like you do when you get off the roller coaster. My ears are ringing.

God, what was that? Jeannine says, breathing hard.

God? Johnny says. God's pulling the str-r-r-r-ings on our car.

What? I ask Lion.

Pfff, he says, brushing the air with his hand, Johnny's nuts. That's all.

It *is* pretty weird, this hill.

That old mine up there makes it happen, Lion says.

There's a mine up there? I say. I didn't know we'd gone so far. They got cars going underground?

No, it's a strip mine. They don't work it anymore.

It's got *magic,* Johnny says.

Lion looks sideways at me, smirks.

Let's go see, I say.

Yeah, sure, Lion says. He turns on the car, shuts off the radio, makes a U-turn. I look back at Jeannine. Johnny's got his arms around her, watching her. She's looking at me. Her eyes look slanted, like she's Chinese. They make me feel like I shot her. I turn back around.

At the top of the hill we pull onto this dusty road I didn't see before. We go for a while through woods, the leaves hang so thick over us I can't see the sky. We drive till we come to a clearing where the hills around us are cut open.

By the moonlight you can see the dirt in them is striped — dark light dark light — like slices of layer cake. In the middle of the clearing, on flat ground, there's rusty trucks and broken-down scaffolding and huge mountains of something that looks like sand. Everything sits there, real quiet, like a picture of the world before people, when there was nothing but hairy elephants and giant rocks.

We drive around the piles of sand. What's sand doing here? I ask.

It's not sand, Lion says, it's culm banks from the coal.

I laugh and say, Come banks?

He laughs and says it again. Leftover junk, he says, they call it waste, and it's no good, they'd flush it down a toilet if they had one big enough.

What color is it? I say. You can't tell in the dark.

It's gray, not black like coal.

Then he turns off the car. We sit there and look out the front window.

Let's climb one, I say.

Sometimes it's like quicksand. Sometimes people fall in and never come out.

We're quiet for a minute. Then I say, Let's go for it.

Wait, Jeannine says.

I get out of the car, slam the door, walk over to the largest pile. Behind me I hear a door open. Lion comes up from behind, puts his arm around my shoulder. We stand in front of a pile, I have to tip my head back to see to the top. The moon's right there, balancing on the tip of the mound, and it's like if you climbed to the top you could touch it.

I put my foot on the culm. I expect it'll be soft like sand. But it's hard. Hard as rock. Maybe it's been sitting around too long. Maybe it needs to be walked on.

I'm going up, I say, and I step away from Lion.

After a few seconds, he follows.

We should feel it out before we put our feet down, he says.

Yeah, I say, stepping higher, fast as I'd walk stairs.

We don't have to go all the way, he says.

I know, I say, fixing my eyes on the top.

The air's cooled off. In the moonlight, the culm doesn't look gray, it looks white. When I glance at my sandals, I can't tell where my feet end and the culm begins, that's what color it is.

The pile's steep and we're getting up high, higher than the trees. Lion's breathing heavy, I listen and I hear that I am too. Also I hear voices, down on the ground, in the car. They go loud then soft then loud again, like ambulances when they're far away.

This is easy, Lion says, if I'd known this, I would of gone up here sooner.

It's cake, I say. Nothing to it.

I'm feeling my lungs fill up with night sky. I look at him. He's sweating, some of his hair sticks to his cheeks. I turn away, close my eyes for a second, breathe in deep. I touch my face, and I'm not sweating, not at all. When we get to the top, I'll take his hand and put it on my face. He won't even know it's summer.

I'm just about to say, Race you to the top, when from down below I hear *Get out!* real loud. It's Jeannine's voice. The car door slams, the engine roars up.

We turn and look as the car screeches away, around the piles of culm, down the road into the woods. Dust flies everywhere, and as it settles, there's Johnny, sitting in the dirt. Even from this high up we can hear him wail like a baby.

Hey, Johnny, Lion calls, taking a couple steps down, what the hell happened?

She thr-r-r-r-ew me out! he says.

Ha! Jeannine's learning. I smile.

You all right? he shouts.

Yeah, Johnny whimpers.

He's all right, I say, and I put my hand on Lion's arm. She probably went to get beer. Let's keep going.

Lion glances at me, then shouts down, She say she'd come back?

She said she never wanted to see any of us again.

She never *what?* She has my car!

He starts running down the hill, in steps so big I think his legs'll split apart.

I stand and yell after him, I'm staying up here.

Suit yourself, he says without breaking his stride.

At the bottom, he runs to Johnny, picks him up off the ground, puts his arm around him. They bend toward each other and talk low.

Who cares. They're a pair of idiots. It's good Jeannine finally learned something. No more little girl crap. She couldn't of done it without me. She's driving home now, tomorrow she'll say thanks. I'll hitch back, I'll find my way, I'll make it somehow. I always do. But — she left me without my purse in God-knows-where. I don't even know what county I'm in.

I turn to face the top of the pile and start climbing again. The culm sparkles, I hadn't noticed that before, it's made of little black diamonds. I step hard. I'm gonna check the world out from the top, make this night worth *some*thing. My feet slap down, the boys talk below, crickets are everywhere.

Then, no warning — my foot breaks through the hard crust and sinks in, up to my thigh. My other leg bends, at the knee, my hands push out in front of me, I gotta keep myself from falling in, keep myself back.

For a second I forget to breathe.

Then I realize it's not sucking me in deeper, it's not pull-ing. It's holding me, tight, like I've fallen into the finger of a giant glove. The funny thing is, it's not cold or prickly. I can't feel it at all — it's as if the culm and my leg are the same thing.

I try to lift myself up, push with my hands. But nothing happens. It's like trying to pull a tree out of the ground.

The moon hangs over my head, high, big. I stop and twist around. The boys are still there. I don't want them to see me stuck like this, but if I don't call out, they might leave without me, and I'll be here all night.

And then they turn from me and start walking away, walking back toward Magnet Hill. I stop and hold perfectly still. They follow the tracks Jeannine made when she took off. She's gotta be miles away by now, hands gripping the wheel, no looking back. Not even for me. Not even think-ing of me. Sweat runs down my face, soaks the ends of my hair. I wipe my eyelids, my face, shake out my wet hands. When I open my eyes, it takes a second to find Lion and Johnny. They're almost into the woods. My chest unlocks like a trap door, and I feel something I've never felt before.

Hey, Lion, I call out. Hey, guys.

They stop moving. Back here, I yell. Lion turns and tugs at his brother, then points up the hill at me.

Come back. Please. I need you, I shout, waving my arms. And I mean it for the first time in my life.

LAUNCHING
THE ECHO

THEY DON'T WANT TO LOOK. They're not even inter-
ested. On one side of us a rock cliff stretches like a gigantic
wall toward the sky, and on the other side a river twists a
mile below the edge of the road. I point out the car window.
"Look, girls," I say to my daughters. "Look at the icicles!
Look at how fast the river's flowing!" But they sit back, all
three of them, even the infant, and cross their arms, and
sigh.

"Why'd you turn the radio off, Mommy?" This is the
oldest one talking. When they are trapped in the car, the
radio is what matters, that and a storybook for her, a thumb
for the middle one, and my breast for the baby.

"I had to," I tell her.

"But *why?*"

"Too much interference."

"How long till the sound comes back?"

"About thirty minutes."

"No!" the two older girls cry. "Aaaa!" the baby adds.

Every week, the same conversation. This keeps our minds
off what we drive away from on the weekends. What we
drive away from is my second husband, the father of the
baby. I've come to realize he is not the best man to live

with. He stews in his Krishna consciousness, praying to his shrine, dressing the deities before he goes to bed. He waits for me to come home Sunday nights to pick his clothes off the floor and make his lunch for the week. But he is a little better than the man before him, the father of my middle girl. I never married that one. He helped around the house, though he made more work in the process; the philosophy of recycling guided his every move, and so he refused to allow paper products, such as bathroom tissue, to be delicate about it, in the house. But I must admit that both men were better than my first husband. In my memory, he has a snout, to facilitate barking. If I disobeyed his instructions — written in list form when he left for work — he would punish me by staying out until his girlfriends brushed on their morning make-up and skipped off to school.

I believe my girls do not know that I have a weakness for bad men. They certainly do not know how easily the touch of a man's hand on my skin and the sight of his eyes when I feel he loves me can eclipse my common sense. All they know is that there have been a few daddies in their lives, and that money is necessarily preceded by "not enough." And that the daddy who is there now, who I have finally asked to leave but who probably won't unless I throw him out physically, responds to them with little more than silence.

And so, every weekend, I drive. I pack the cooler, bundle the girls up, strap them into their kiddie seats. I set up the oldest girl with Dr. Seuss and coloring books, the middle one with hand puppets, and the baby with an assortment of plastic toys. Then I click on the radio and we roll onto the highway, and in four hours we are at my mother's house, where there are no men.

After the radio scatters to static, we sing songs. "Jingle Bells" was number one on this hit parade for a while. Then "Rudolph," and then "Yellow Submarine."

Today the last remains of winter are melting. Streams of water course down the cliff icicles like tears. The ice upstream has broken up, and the river splashes wild as it finally bursts out of the restraints of cold weather. I watch the world around me, crack open the window, and inhale cool air, the smell of clean dirt. The older girls play in the back. The infant fidgets beside me, calling out her favorite and only word, "Aaaa."

I start them into "This Land Is Your Land." They know the words. It comes easily and fast. We're going along, the baby's aaaaing right with us, we sound just great — and in the middle of the chorus I realize that their lead has drifted away; I have stopped singing.

"What's the matter, Mommy?" the oldest says as the ribbon of their voices begins to fray.

I barely hear her at first. The faces of my husbands and lovers are parading by the windshield, along with memories of resolutions I made, then broke. Always, I seize the first hand that offers to haul me out of a pit, then cling to that hand until it tosses me into the next pit. And then, beaten down and empty, I eagerly reach out for more of the same.

"Mommy, are you OK?" the middle one says. "Why are you crying?"

"Because it's so beautiful outside," I tell them.

"It's boring," the oldest one says.

Up ahead I see a lookout point. Fourteen times in the last two months I have passed by that point, wondering what it would be like to stop there, get out, and stand at the railing. The ground drops away there, and the valley stretches so far it seems like the whole world.

"What're we doing?"

"I want to stop so we can look over the valley."

"How come?"

"It'll be fun. We'll just stop for a minute."

Even the baby is quiet as I pull onto the gravel and park.

The two older girls let themselves out. I unbuckle the baby and take her in my arms.

All four of us stand at the railing. We are in the elbow of a cliff that rises both behind us and to our left. To our right is the valley. The river snakes below us to the horizon. Along the banks of the water cluster the pink and yellow pastels of early spring. Patches of fields cut through the puffs of trees, and specks that must be houses dot the sides of roads.

The girls' eyes open wide. "Wow," the older ones say.

Standing here, the two voices come out rich and full, and return to us in an echo.

"Did you hear that?" they ask me.

"Hear what?"

"This." And they shout again: "Wow!"

"Yes," I say, as the echo begins. "I hear it."

"Wow!" they yell out. "Wow! Wow!" Their voices come back to us like waves at the ocean, rolling over and over until you can't tell the original from the sounds they've caused.

Then they look at me. "Mommy," they say, and they pull at my jacket. "You shout something."

"No, I'll just listen," I say.

"Please?" they say. "Please?"

"I don't want to."

"Come on." And they give me no peace until I agree and open my mouth.

I am not planning what I'll say. It just comes out like some part of me passing through to the outside, like when my voice is at rest in my sadder moods, and this is the shape it finds itself in.

"Mmmmm-en!" I shout. The older girls giggle, the baby claps her hands. And my voice ripples back across the valley.

At my side, the older girls join in with the fading trace

of my voice. "Men!" they shout. "Mmmmm-en!" The baby joins in. "Aaaa!" They're all going, their voices filling up the valley. And finally I join back in. "Men!" we shout together. "Mmmmm-en!"

Our voices layer into each other. I look at them and notice their huge grins and how this shouting together makes them jump up and down. Someday my girls will have their own histories with men. I wonder if this memory will make them smile then.

THE SECRET LIVES
OF MY TOYS

WHEN I WAS SEVEN years old, my parents insisted that I join the Brownies.

My older sister was a Brownie and through them had, for the first time in her life, found friends who liked her as much as she liked them. The change was remarkable; you can see it in the pictures: the little girl behind thick, vulture-eyed glsses, her face sagging like melted putty, suddenly, at the first Brownie barbecue, draws herself up and learns to smile. She poses with her arms thrown around her new friends. Her cheeks are red from laughter, her eyes wet from happiness. Even the frames of her glasses seem to sparkle in the afternoon sun.

My parents felt that I could benefit similarly from the Brownies. I did not agree.

My sister had always wanted friends but had been too shy to initiate anything. *I* wasn't afraid to make friends — at least I thought so at the time. I was, I thought, just someone who preferred being alone, because by myself I could do whatever I wanted.

Every afternoon, all the neighborhood kids except me made an exodus to the woods down the street, where they did whatever it was that kids did together. During these afternoons, I would run from one yard to the next, sampling different swing sets. Eventually, I would match the seat of my pants to the seat of some worn swing, and then take off into the air, swinging so high that I would be enveloped by autumn leaves the color of candy corn, or winter branches stretching out to embrace me, or the soothing green fans of spring and summer.

While I swung, I made up long, rambling songs about the secret lives of my toys. In my songs, my dolls and stuffed animals came alive and danced through the neighborhood. My toys could go inside every basement and attic and tree; they knew no boundaries. They took me along. We liked all the same things. We never fought, and they listened to and appreciated everything I confided in them. Together we shared many secret adventures.

At night, my toys and I played alone in my room. We kept the door closed so that we wouldn't have to include anyone else. I came out only to eat dinner. Television did not interest me. Other children did not interest me. And I knew, long before my parents forced me to join, that the Brownies would not interest me either.

The Brownies had vows, traditions, group activities, drab uniforms. Every Thursday, we were marched down the school hallway by our two troop leaders and assembled in the gymnasium. There we were indoctrinated with the customs and lore of the Brownies. On the day of the initiation pledge, I deliberately held up my left hand instead of my right, knowing that to do so would be considered blasphemous. One girl poked me, but I droned on woodenly with the pledge. At last a cry rose up from the suddenly attentive troop leaders, and, just before I finished, a pair of stiff, older hands jerked down the offending arm and cranked up the proper one.

I begged my parents to let me leave the Brownies. "But

look at your sister," my mother said, "she's being invited to parties now. Don't you want to be invited to parties?" "No," I mumbled, but I knew it was no good. They'd enlisted me and expected me to stay until my tour of duty was up.

In the meantime, I was dragged along on Brownie trips. Zoos, museums, historical sights — I passed through all in my paper-thin regulation Brownie uniform, standing away from the group, shaking my head yes or no if anyone spoke to me, yawning every few minutes.

There is only one trip that made any real impression. It sits as clearly in my mind as the photographs of my sister.

One day, in the fall of second grade, the Brownie troop leaders gathered us up after school and drove us in their two station wagons to a neighboring town. There we wound our way through a residential area, an older kind, like the one where I lived, the kind where every house is unique and well groomed, and all the hedges are meticulously clipped. I imagined running around these lawns in the late afternoons, trying out the swing sets I saw in the backyards.

The sky, when we got out of the cars, was layered like gelatin pudding, in pink, purple, and blue. The first star was out. The streetlights popped on. The lawns around us were so well trimmed that they looked like drawings.

We were led by our troop leaders across a quiet street to a small house and ushered through the back door into the kitchen. There, in the bright light, we met the owner, Mr. Edgerton, the tallest and thinnest man I had ever seen. Mr. Edgerton was so tall, his neck curled over like the top of a lowercase letter *f*. He smiled as if we were presents someone had given him for Christmas and thanked us again and again for coming. As he passed around a plate of cookies he said he'd made just for us, I slipped into the living room to see if anyone else was home. It didn't seem likely; aside from the kitchen, the house was as dark as the space between my dreams.

Then Mr. Edgerton led us downstairs into his basement.

There, by the light of a single bulb, we saw an enormous table, so large it almost filled the whole room. On top of the table was a miniature, handcrafted town. There were houses, each lit from the inside, streets, cars, a glittering river, a park, a trolley, grass, trees, flowers. There were also little people, each no bigger than my middle finger, positioned throughout the whole scene. Some rode the cars and trolley, some ate dinner or watched television in their houses, some just stood in midstep along the streets. All were thin. All wore the same blank expression on their faces, as though they had fallen asleep with their eyes open.

The Brownies circled the table. From what I knew of the world, Mr. Edgerton had every detail right, from the letters on the marquee of the movie house to the pails in the sand-boxes. There were also things I barely knew, like an or-chestra in the outdoor theater, scullers on the river, a funeral at the cemetery. I wanted to touch everything to make sure it was real, and I wanted to be tiny, like the little people, so I could live in this town, too.

Then our troop leaders directed our attention back to Mr. Edgerton. "Isn't this something," they said. "And he did this all by himself."

Our host grinned so hard I thought his face would crack open.

"And look," they added, as he lowered his head with modesty, "he doesn't even have five fingers, like the rest of us. Just look at his hands."

Mr. Edgerton held up his hands, and, though they were the size of normal hands, each hand had only two fingers. The fingers were twice the size of any fingers I'd seen, and they resembled a thumb and a pinky pointing in opposite directions, as if they were on a clock that read quarter to three. The palm in the middle was small, little more than a hinge to hold the thumb and pinky together. He wiggled his fingers at us. I looked down at my own hands. I tried to imagine making this whole world with only four fingers, but I couldn't. I couldn't even imagine holding on to swings.

When I looked back at him, Mr. Edgerton had picked up one of the little people and was fondling it between the two fingers of his right hand. He gazed down at it, still with his smile, and then beyond his hand to the little town. As he took it all in, the look on his face reminded me more than anything ever had and ever would of the look on my sister's face in the barbecue pictures.

It was a moment before I realized that I had covered my mouth with my hand. Had my face ever looked like that when I played with my toys? I started to think so, but I couldn't be sure.

The troop leaders announced that it was time to go, and one by one, the Brownies followed them up the stairs. As I, the last girl to leave, got halfway up the stairs, I looked down at Mr. Edgerton.

There he was, still beaming at his town on the table, the town that now seemed, from my position alone on the stairs, terribly small.

Mr. Edgerton glanced up and saw me watching him. We stood and stared at each other, and, even in the dim light, I could see crimson roll into his face. Finally, he lowered his head. "I'm sorry," he said, gently placing the little person back on the table, "I didn't realize you'd all gone up already."

I watched him make his way around the table. Then, just as he reached out for the bannister, I spun around, leaving him behind, and scrambled up the stairs.

The other girls laughed when I burst through the doorway

into the kitchen. I ignored them and bolted my way around their starched brown uniforms to the back of the room.

The air was crisp and the sky completely dark when the troop leaders dropped me off at my house. I opened the front door. My parents were sitting beside each other on the sofa, watching television. They were holding hands in a lazy, casual way, as though it was something they did all the time. Maybe it was.

"Did you have fun?" my mother said when I closed the door.

"It was fine," I replied. I sat at the foot of the stairs and unlaced my shoes. My parents were both watching me, their eyebrows arched, as if poised for disappointment. On the television in front of them, a family of attractive people muttered and giggled. My father patted the sofa. "You might like this," he said. I looked at his hand, and at the hollow in the cushion beneath it, while upstairs my toys rustled in the darkness of my room, distressed I hadn't gone to see them as soon as I'd come home.

SHEETS

ALVINA WOULD WALK through the wall, if she could. Step halfway in — one arm, one leg. Just far enough to reach that whimpering child in the row house next door. She'd pluck the girl from her bed — Alvina knows where the bedroom is. She wouldn't be caught. Day and night, she hears the girl's mother twaddling on the phone in another room, cracking her gum in front of the television. Never knows what the child's doing.

Alvina would rescue the girl. Ronnie, that's her name. She'd carry her back here, cuddle her in these brown arms, press her to this worn face, to the skin with its ripples like soft desert sand. She could have a bed ready in a minute, a second. That one, over there. The one her husband used to sleep in before his cough got the better of him.

Behind the house, cars whistle past on the expressway. Cats scurry by the chain link fence between the tiny yards. She hears them now, matted fur strumming the dull steel like a toneless harp. Once she took in a tabby she found dizzy and tangled after a fight. The pads of its feet were as shredded as old ballet slippers, and one of its eyes was missing. She dribbled iodine on its wounds, fed it milk through an eyedropper. In a month it slipped through a hole in the screen. She hears it sometimes, at night. It screams as if it's in a tunnel so dark, its single eye cannot find the exit.

Ronnie plays in the dirt out back, summer and winter. Her toys are plastic milk jugs, strips of curtain lining, egg cartons. She keeps a dirt collection. With a fork she digs out little pieces from all over the project, up and down the strip backing onto the highway, then stores the dirt in the foam pouches of the cartons. "What'cha doing?" Alvina asked her once, leaning over the chain link fence.

"I'm a dirt scientist," Ronnie said. "I'm getting dirt from everybody's backyard."

Alvina asked to see. Ronnie held up her egg carton. Each sample was labeled in a child's scrawl. "All the times of the year. From my house to the end of the street." She said it with pride.

"What'cha looking for in it?"

"Color. Smell. Different stuff. See, this one's red, this one's got Coke cans, this one had worms in it — only they ain't there no more."

"You dig up mud?"

"Yeah. I like when it's hard and old and got cracks like an earthquake. See, this one's cracked. But you wouldn't know about it now. In this box, it looks just like all the other ones."

Days, Alvina goes to the library. She can read, but she does not want to; it is more interesting to watch the people. Lovers amble past looking at each other, their bodies breathing silent ballads together. Young women shuffle through the stacks, clasping ringed fingers over their swelling waistlines. Mothers kneel onto the dusty granite, buttoning the jackets of their small children.

Alvina sits at the same table every day, the one farthest from the vagrants, who pack themselves onto sofas in the sun room. Alvina does not want to be confused with them. She bathes every morning before leaving the house, irons her dresses, combs her white hair.

She does not watch soap operas. She has no television.

She sweeps the apartment every morning, every evening. She polishes the thief bars on her windows once a week.

At night, boys with radios the size of houses pass by, one after another. Big boys, testing out the fusing of their bones, the hardening of their muscles. Dark as starless nights. The same boys who only last year stood beside the highway and threw stones at the cars of white people. Now, they bribe girls with their radios. "Hey, what's up. Let's dance in the street." Even in winter. Boys and girls leap about on the frozen street in front of the project, breaking up only for the occasional rattletrap. They jump high, they roll around; hot and flushed, they look the way she felt when she was their age.

Alvina's curtains have moth holes. The hems have frayed. She combs the loose threads to make them hang straight.

She wishes they'd had children. She wishes Arnel hadn't put off adopting. She waits for her Social Security check in the mail.

When the ice storm comes that winter, it slicks the dirt out back like a white mirror. The world outside is crystal. Even loose garbage in the yard glistens. Before her head leaves the pillow, Alvina can tell by the flat silence that the expressway is closed.

At her back widow, shielding her eyes from the sun, Alvina sees Ronnie. The girl is crouching beside the fence, jabbing at the ice with a fork in one hand, holding an open egg carton with the other. Alvina throws on her sweaters, buttons up her coat, steps outside.

"Collecting ice now?"

Ronnie looks up. "Yeah. I'm seeing if ice dirt's like regular dirt."

"That can't be fun."

"It's *fun*," Ronnie says, breaking one section into several small chunks of ice. She picks up one with a brown center as if it's a diamond, holds it up to the sky, grins. After a minute, she puts it in the egg carton.

"Highway's closed," Alvina says.

"I know."

Alvina looks away, to the strip of road behind her house, where for years she has seen cars, baked silver by the sun, streaking by like schools of fish. Now it's like the river's been drained dry; all she can see is the bottom, and the fish have melted into a big sheet that stretches over the riverbed as far as she can see.

"I'm gonna take me a stroll down the highway," Alvina says. "Never know when this'll happen again."

Ronnie looks up, her hands wrapped around the fork handle.

"You coming with me?" Alvina asks.

The girl glances back at her mother's house. Through the plastic on the broken kitchen window drifts the low, deep chatter of white men on the television and her mother's high voice weaving through theirs as she gossips on the phone. The quiet of the expressway makes Alvina feel as if she's in the country again. Cars there were such strangers, years after Alvina moved north she kept confusing distant horns with the cries of tired babies. Ronnie's visited the country only once that Alvina can think of. The girl's never lived in a home where if no one's talking she hears silence. Alvina says, "This like that school trip to the state park you liked so much? No people, no sounds?" Ronnie turns and faces the expressway and lowers the egg carton to the ground. "Yeah," she says.

The little girl climbs over the fence, then holds open a small flap in the steel for Alvina to crawl through. On the other side, they step carefully around naked hedges, and step out onto the shoulder.

The light along the highway is blinding, as though all the spotlights in the world were turned on them. Alvina squints, and tears slip away from her eyes. Ronnie runs on ahead. In this light, on this ice, the little girl looks blacker than the blackest marble. She skips and slides along the road.

Alvina watches and follows behind and thinks to herself: she looks like the shadow of a flame.

I'll always be here to catch her if she falls.

★   ★   ★

Before the projects, before the first gray hair. Long, long ago. Alvina is new to the city.

Clear nights on the roof, Alvina can see so many stars she feels as if someone spilled a box of sugar across the sky. She and Arnel live right underneath, in a one-room attic apartment. Its ceiling hangs low; at night it seems to wrap around their bed. On the roof they found a pair of wooden chairs. Alvina scrubbed the soot off, set them up for a good view. Every night she and Arnel have free they leave that room, sit under the stars and look out to the city.

Arnel plays his banjo, the round box an oat can, the neck a broom handle. He picks at the strings, plink, plunk, as he serenades the city. Alvina sits beside him, reading library books or just gazing. The city spreads before them like a blanket of lights; sometimes she feels she could stretch out her arm and grab one, hold it as it glows in her smooth and unlined hands.

Arnel got into a good job here, loading war weapons in a factory. It's a bustling place; he comes home with his feet sore, in need of rubbing. For Alvina, it's knees and hands that hurt. Her job is in an elegant theater, where she polishes marble and terrazzo floors at night after a ballet. She shows up early sometimes, peers through an open door in the balcony, watches. The dancers are lithe and white and seem to fly. Alvina tries to remember how they move.

Now, on the roof, she practices. Spinning, whirling, up on her toes. Arnel strums a tune and she follows. She tosses her arms this way and that, leaps with legs parted wide. Give her one of the dancers' white ruffled costumes and who could tell the difference.

Sometimes at work, while Alvina's wire brush is arching across the floor in her hand, she hears the ballerinas talking as they pad in twos and threes from the dressing room to the street. They complain their feet hurt, their husbands won't dance — nothing that matters to Alvina. Nothing, that is, until the day she hears them boast about how long each has gone since she bled. Six months, says one. Thirteen, brags another. They one-up each other, making Alvina gasp, because if she were chiming in she'd lose to them all, a simple one month being the longest Alvina's ever had to wait.

Arnel and Alvina have been trying for a baby. Some folks back home had secrets, and Alvina wrote them to get ideas. "Lie with him only when the moon's full," Alvina's aunt scrawled. "Rabbit bones in the bed," Mink the Albino had his brother write. Arnel and Alvina try it all, each idea, but every four weeks her body sends the message that no baby's growing, and even the most guaranteed of tricks can't seem to make that fact change.

Mist lets Alvina's hair untwist itself from her ribbon and sprout. She pats it down as she rides the bus home. Used to be, she walked, but when Arnel took note of her three gray hairs last year, he said, "A young lady like you's got no business getting gray," and told her she ought to start riding the bus.

Tonight, the air is thick enough to see; the sky looks close, a big gray hat resting on top of the street. Alvina squints through the mist as she steps off the bus. Inside the front door stands Arnel, peering up like he's reading flaking paint on the wall. She can see through the glass he's whistling.

He opens the door wearing that smile he has, half a halo swung low. "Some buddies from work're upstairs," he says. The war over, he's in a store now, asking, Floor, please? in an elevator paneled with rosewood, mirrors, and the perfumes of shopping women. "They came to see our new radio."

Radio's almost all they own, except for the bed and kitchenware. It's squat as a fat woman, sits in their room at the foot of the bed. Bathroom's smaller than the radio, probably.

Tunes from their place toot down the stairs. Arnel's banging at doors on the way, laughing. Neighbors open up, poke faces into the stairwell. "Party at our place, friends!" Arnel says, rapping on the next door. Some folks close back up, but most step out and take hold of the bannister.

Upstairs, guests pile onto the mattress, crowd along the walls, everyone's singing along. Alvina has some pie she sets out, and one of the men brought wine. Arnel, pouring some in a glass for Alvina, leans forward and whispers, "My cousin says he'll send his boy to come live with us, if we tell him yes. When he starts school. Maybe we'll have us a child after all."

Just then the Duke comes on the radio and Arnel slides his arm around Alvina's waist, draws her into the doorway, and they dance. So many people so close heat up the air, and in the dark bedroom window lit from the inside Alvina sees her face, glowing like black fire. Arnel holds his arm high, and Alvina underneath it twirls. She spots like a ballerina, looking at Arnel, whipping her head around quick, looking at Arnel again. All kinds of faces are in the room: old, adult, young. Faster and faster she goes until the ages blur together; until all the faces streaking past come to seem like one.

Nighttime, and rain slaps against the side of the theater. It is quiet, except for the rat-a-tat-tat of the water. Alvina packs away her brush and bucket for the night and coats her hands with Vaseline. Years of soap water have made her knuckles thick and cracked; sometimes the pink side of her fingers gives out and splits wide open. Tonight she makes her way along the upstairs corridor to the stairway. The dancers have already left; there is nothing to see but the hallway and the fire escape outside. She shuffles past the windows, not taking note, and then something out the glass stops her, turns her around to look.

A teenage girl, maybe thirty years younger than Alvina, is sitting on the metal landing. She is hugging her legs in close, resting her arms on her knees, and burying her face in the sloped lap. The girl's hair melts down her dark cheeks in the rain, and her eyes are shut. Her dress clings to her; every curve shows.

Alvina stands watching the girl in the rain. Then she pushes up the window. The clatter of water on the metal staircase echoes in the theater corridor. "What're you doing?"

The girl turns her head without lifting it and glances at the window, her face so blank it's as if the rain had washed her away. Alvina knows she does not work here; she must have climbed up from the ground. The girl looks back down to her bent knees.

"Didn't you hear me?"

"Go away." The girl talks into her legs.

"You can't keep sitting there getting wet," Alvina says, and this time the girl doesn't even look up.

Alvina rests on one knee on the windowsill and tests the rain. It is so cold that she thinks it'll soon switch to hail. But what's she going to do — leave that girl out there? Alvina pulls herself outside. The rain thumps onto her like a jazz pianist's hands.

She shoves the window closed, then sits against the railing. The girl, head down this whole time, peeks out an eye. "What're you doing here, lady?"

The water has beaten the air out of Alvina's dress and now the cloth is slicked on like skin. "I figure anybody sitting out in the rain must be needing some company."

The girl picks her head up, and she and Alvina face each other. Alvina can see over the girl's shoulder. A bus passes by. Women cloaked in furs huddle beneath awnings. Raindrops fall through the dark and in the light from the theater become speckles of white, then strike the street and are swallowed back into black.

"I've got a problem," the girl says finally. It's been at least ten minutes that they've been facing each other. She drops her hands to her stomach and curls her fingers over the roundness. "I don't want no baby."

Alvina sees this every week with the girls on her block. "Can't expect it'll go away," Alvina says. "Don't you have a mother or a grandma you can look to for help?"

"No."

"Well, you got to find somebody to care for it."

The girl, a frown set deeper than her age should allow, sighs heavily and says, "You want it?"

For a wild flash Alvina thinks of putting the question to Arnel, but she knows he'll say they can't take on kids, same as he says when Alvina brings up the neighborhood girls; the cot's already earmarked. "My husband and I, we're waiting to adopt a boy from home."

"A little baby?"

"No, he must be fourteen, fifteen by now. His father's had to keep him around for family help, but he should be coming soon."

The girl smirks and shakes her head. "You think they'll send him off at that age? Ha."

Alvina used to ask Arnel this very question, but with his cough getting worse lately, she's let off. What would be the use? Every year they said they'd send the boy, and every year, because of money problems or someone getting sick, they didn't. Still, Alvina keeps hoping. "Well," she says, "let's put our heads together. Maybe I can help you come up with a person who'd want it."

"I can't think of a single soul," the girl says.

Alvina can imagine all kinds of people who might help. Sisters, aunts, friends. Could even be a neighbor the girl isn't remembering right now. Alvina will come up with an answer. Alvina will stay here until she and the girl can figure it out. "I bet there is."

"What's it to you anyway?" the girl says, looking at the theater window, then back at Alvina. "Why do you care?"

Alvina makes fists of her rough hands and shoves them against the seams of her pockets. The rain is so heavy, so cold, it pounds to the inside of her bones.

"Because," she says.

★   ★   ★

Winter, seventy years before the projects. Alvina in a backyard of grass. Grass covered with ice.

Alvina is on the back porch of her first house, the real house in the country, where the other side of walls is the outside; where streets serve mostly as beds for sleepy dogs. She ties her shoes, her long black hair hanging in braids. She is small and soft, her skin as smooth as the tide sand on a beach. After she buttons her coat all the way to the top, Alvina climbs down the long wooden stairway, leaving her mother upstairs beside the changing table, powder in one hand, her brother's tiny feet in the other, woman and baby giggling with each other.

Outside — where are the others? Mary, Paula, Jamie? Not a single foot has hollowed a print in the ice. Not a single voice cuts through the wooo of the wind. Mothers hold all the children indoors, let them touch no more than the cold glass of the windows. "It's too icy out there, you best not go for you fall and crack your head open."

But what they are missing! The world is Alvina's. She skates across the iced lawn, gliding over blades of grass, frozen insects, sleeping worms. Arms out, she keeps her balance. When she slows down, she runs a few yards, then stops, and lets the ghost of her running feet carry her along. This way and that. Back and forth across the lawn until it seems she's worn it all down.

Then she steps heavily, digging her feet into the ice near her neighbor's picket fence. The ice here is thin. Her footsteps leave patterns like spiderwebs.

She finds the hole in the fence, crawls through. This is where Miss Lela Jackson lives. The richest black lady you'll ever know. Lives right next door on enough land for three families, with a backyard that slopes down so far, it could be a sledding hill. Somehow she got it all from a white man. Gray hair sticks out from her head like a fistful of snakes. She screams if you step on her lawn. She bumps into folks she doesn't like when they're carrying big packages, and laughs when the apples scatter and the eggs break.

Always, always, Miss Lela hangs laundry outside. She

seems to live for laundry. From Alvina's house you can see Miss Lela's kitchen, where that thick little body steams over the washboard, that chubby little hand wipes a trickle of sweat off her forehead. Then — the squeal of the clothesline as she reels it in, the click-click of clothespins as she hangs dresses, blouses, stockings, on the rope. The rope now covered with ice. She's left everything up since yesterday. Her sheets have turned into walls.

Alvina steps onto Miss Lela's lawn. Fresh ice. As clean and untouched as the newly polished floor at the house Alvina's mother cleans. Alvina looks up to the back of the house. No lights. No head in the window.

And so, onto the hill. Swoop like a bird. Circle round the clothes, they hang stiff and low. She glides around some trousers, turns, then swings back around a nightgown, then back again. Down the hill, weaving in and out, around and around. She's a real ice skater. She's like the high school girls on the pond. Spinning, sliding, laughing, in the pure, clean air.

But the bottom of the hill comes too fast. Her toes lift up, her heels dig in — then flip, over and under. She lands on her face.

All the world goes still. It practically buzzes with silence. She turns over, opens her eyes — and everything has turned white.

Up — the sky is white.

Down — her body is white.

Across the lawn — the way to her house, the way up the hill — all white. Solid as rock.

She picks herself up, puts out her arms in front of her. If I go way up, I'll be on that hill. On that hill I can find the fence. Then the hole. Then I'll be right home with my mama.

But the sharp edge of an iced sheet almost splits her in

two. She moves to the side, tries to walk, one foot in front of the other. Steps carefully, heavily — and slam! hits another sheet broadside. Her feet just won't move straight.

She sits down and cries. A breeze picks up and blows away her hat. Her eyes are so cold.

Suddenly an arm tugs at her. "Quit your howling," Miss Lela says. "What're you doing here?"

"I fell and now I can't see!" Alvina looks in the direction of Miss Lela. All that's there is white.

"What'cha mean, you can't see? Your eyes they look fine."

"They ain't fine. Would I be walking into sheets if they was?"

Miss Lela says nothing. Alvina wonders if she'll get punished, if Miss Lela will pin her on the clothesline so she'll freeze like a gingerbread girl. No one ever comes in this yard. Who would know, till she thawed in the spring?

Then Alvina feels the palm of a glove take her mittened hand. "This way. This way. Up here, up, up. Careful. This way. One foot after another — watch your stepping."

That foot up, this one higher — yes, stairs. Inside. Mothballs and linseed oil and bacon and cider. "Lie down here."

Something scratchy and warm on her face.

"Shoot, girl, you know what you got wrong? You got ice in your eyes."

Miss Lela lifts the towel from Alvina's eyes a little bit at a time, like it's a kettle lid and she wants to see if the water's boiling. Slowly, the white begins to melt at the edges. She takes the towel away. Alvina tries to see.

Ceiling beams.

Oil paintings.

Lace curtains.

The ice swims around, giving Alvina a glimpse of this,

a glance at that. Miss Lela's face appears, then falls behind the ice. It's like there's a moving wall in Alvina's eyes.

Finally it breaks apart. The tiny crystals make the world look as though it is full of white holes, like the world is something that comes only in pieces.

At last, even the tiny crystals melt.

Miss Lela brings Alvina a bracelet, a string of pink and white beads only big enough for a doll, or a baby. "Why don't you have this?" she says. "My little girl can't use it no more."

"I never seen a little girl here."

"She ain't around no more."

Alvina puts on her coat. They walk next door, around the front way. They ring the bell. Miss Lela clutches Alvina's hand. They wait for the weatherworn door to swing open.

"I've been watching you," Miss Lela says, peering down at Alvina. "You need to be more careful."

"Will you take care of me again? Like if I fall, will you help?"

"You best be careful you don't."

"I can't help it if I do."

Miss Lela sighs. Footsteps come up to the other side of the door. "Maybe I'll help you," she says. "But don't be expecting too much of me."

"I won't," Alvina says. "And I'll do something nice for you in return."

"Like what? I don't need nothing."

"I don't know right now," Alvina says, looking up at Miss Lela's face. "Give me time. Let me think."

AFTERGLOW

WHEN MADELINE first came here from her aunt's house, her pop asked her politely to help out with the cleaning, but this had changed lately. Now she couldn't be bothered with cleaning. A thirteen-year-old could at least make her own bed, was what her stepmother, Hilda Gail, was probably thinking. But Madeline couldn't see taking the time to pull the bedspread taut and neat, the hem equally far from the floor all around. Or wash the dishes or set the storm window into the back door. It was tough getting her point across at first: Madeline sitting knees to chin in a chair, reading, her pop stepping around to the front, saying, I would very much like it if you swept the kitchen floor this week. Maybe, Madeline would say, hitching her book in closer. He would slink away, taking Hilda Gail's elbow, saying, I think I got through. Which made it hard to walk past Hilda Gail to get a snack, with her grading papers at the kitchen table, right next to the broom and all.

But ever since two weeks ago when Madeline hit on this idea of telling them that she had a bun in the oven, everything had become a whole lot easier. Kick the blankets off the bed and leave them in a heap. Hang the dresses on the bedpost and wear them till they keep her shape. Pop didn't care. Hilda Gail didn't seem to either. Pop asking all the time, You all right, Madeline? You feeling OK? No, Madeline would say, and then flop on the sofa or truck into the bathroom. Used to be, Pop and Hilda Gail got the monopoly in the john every morning. Not anymore. Now it was Madeline — running the bath while the water was still hot, soaking it up, checking out Harlequin romances even when someone knocked on the door and asked if please, could they get a few minutes before they had to leave for work. Oh, I feel so lousy, Madeline would say, and they'd walk off and leave her alone. She'd keep reading till she got to a chapter end. Lush gardens and kisses in the rain, men whose gentility belied their real passion, and all the while Madeline sighing at the thought of having a beau of her own someday.

Pop bought her bath crystals yesterday. Keep that skin soft, he said. Hilda Gail — God rest her soul — told him to do it. Madeline had her ear to the wall, so she heard everything. Evan, Hilda Gail said, we're only a few months into this parenting business, but if there's one thing I've learned about as a schoolteacher it's pregnant girls. You have to be kind and treat them well. Look at what's just happened to their lives.

All I know, Pop said back to her, is that my little baby has got herself in trouble, and that the fellow responsible has not called here once. I don't even know who he is.

Let her tell us when she's ready, Hilda Gail said. It was probably hard enough for her to tell us about the child. The girl's got too much to deal with right now, just settling into living here, let alone having to explain all kinds of embarrassing things.

Then what should I do? Pop asked.

Have sympathy, Hilda Gail answered.

So Pop bought Madeline the bath crystals. And he got her tapes of oceans rolling in and out, and a carton of canned bread, which Madeline loved but Hilda Gail thought was a defilement of food, only she got generous and let Madeline have it because, Now's the time to be nice to her, you know. And Pop got lavender potpourri for her room, and a pillowcase of slippery material — ice green, the color of mint chocolate chip, which he was also stocking now. Plus Pop said the days Madeline was too sick in the morning, she coud bag school if she wanted. And you can bet that she was sick every morning, this one being no exception.

Now Madeline was downstairs, surveying the living room mess. Pop had asked her to try cleaning when the morning sickness passed, but of course she wouldn't. Instead, she'd been cutting the handsomest men out of magazines and sticking them in her private folders so she could have somebody new to gaze at before she went to bed. Slick magazine pages lay scattered across the folding table between the kitchen and living room. And everywhere, the usual: dishes, junk mail, soiled clothes, dust.

Madeline snapped on the TV in the living room and the one in the kitchen and turned them to different shows. She liked spending her mornings that way. Lots of times you could get a rhythm going — the folks on one show talking low when the ones on the other were shouting. Back and forth.

She was scooping out some mint chocolate chip when the doorbell rang. Though she couldn't see the front door from where she sat, she knew it was her neighbor Mrs. Lubbock, come to give her some flack but from the civilized entrance instead of the back door, the old busybody so dearly loved to use. Every day Mrs. Lubbock eyed her when Madeline looked back to check out the Pennsylvania Railroad passing by, with its rusted cars of ore and coal, its good-looking engineers waving to her out the window, and in the two weeks since the maternity dresses had become Madeline's daily attire there came from Mrs. Lubbock a harangue Madeline now knew by heart — You should stop lying about your condition, you are taking advantage of a loving father. Madeline listened a couple of times; if there was one thing she had learned in her life, it was that it always pays to know your enemies. The fence between the trains and the row-house yards had blown down in a winter storm a few days ago, which would explain Mrs. Lubbock's coming around to the front today. Of course, Madeline had heard enough of Mrs. Lubbock by now, so she just kept scooping the ice cream while the bell donged to kingdom come. She set herself up at the folding table, where she could see both TVs, and listened to Mrs. Lubbock shuffling around on the front steps, waiting, until finally the feet went away and Madeline was left alone with her scissors and TV and things were as they should be.

Couldn't have been five minutes later, there was a scraping sound at the back door. Squirrels ran near there sometimes and the washing machine made strange noises occasionally, so Madeline didn't pay it any attention. But the sound kept up, like something nibbling, only louder. It wasn't until the nibbling turned into a zipper sound that she caught on it was the screen getting cut. She put down the scissors and slid off the chair and went across the kitchen. At the stove she swung around the corner into the little hallway and felt for a few yards along the dark walls until she came to the washing machine room.

He was just a shadow at first, standing with the light shining through the back door window behind him. Madeline couldn't see a single thing except his outline, and from that little she knew he was not Pop. He was too tall and too thin. His arms hung halfway down his legs; his fingers were long and skinny. He wore a hat that in this light looked like a baseball cap, and from underneath his hair stuck out like it was a bundle of old grass.

176

Madeline thought of asking him, Do you want something, but she knew the words were not going to come, so she stood there in her maternity dress, waiting for his move.

Damn, what are you doing here, girl? the man said. His voice was rough and full of breath, like when the wind blew at night and scraped loose sticks up against the side of the house.

I'm — I'm not feeling right, Madeline said.

That's a shame, the man said. Madeline wanted to see his face, so she would know how he meant that. Behind him the screen door had been sliced open, and then it was just working at the lock on the wood door, she guessed, because that was not open and he was sliding something that looked like a pulled-out paper clip into his pocket. Will you do me a favor? he asked. Madeline nodded. Good. You step back now. Keep your eyes on me and your hands down at your sides.

Madeline did this. Her shoes made a sucking noise when they came off the floor. One foot behind the other. The man stepped toward her, coming away from the sun, and when they passed through the hallway and rounded the corner into the kitchen, she could see him.

His hair was brown and so dirty it had separated into oily strips and his scalp showed. His jaw was huge, maybe as big as half his face, with a brown beard — lighter shade of brown than what was on his head — springing out just faint enough for you to wonder if he'd smeared something over his cheeks by accident. He had on jeans and a jacket missing all its buttons. Underneath was a T-shirt with a picture of a gun on it. The gun was in a bed, and it was smoking a cigarette, and beneath the picture was the word *Afterglow*.

What do you want? Madeline asked. She was backing into the kitchen and could hear the TVs yelling and laughing. Do you want our stuff?

I don't want to steal anything, the man said.

Well, don't you get any ideas about me. I'm pregnant, you know.

He looked her skinny body once over, up and down. She didn't feel the way she sometimes felt with boys. This man's eyes didn't try to see underneath the clothes, but they didn't look at her like a cute little girl either. They seemed to see her like a ladder, maybe, or a rock. Pregnant, huh, he said.

That's right.

He waved a long arm toward the chairs. Sit down, he said.

Madeline backed to the chairs and eased herself into one.

Jesus, he said, noticing both TVs. He snapped the set in the kitchen off. The one in the living room, he watched for a second. Then he picked up the blender and aimed. It was a perfect throw. Glass burst into the room, flew all over the furniture. It tinkled as it settled. That's better, he said, taking a deep breath. He turned to her and grinned.

It was so quiet. No sounds even from outside.

That was the only color set we had, Madeline said.

Too bad, he said. He shrugged, spun around to the refrigerator and pulled the door open. Nice stock, he said, crouching down.

Madeline didn't tell him not to be fooled, that there was mold drilling through most of what was in there.

Where're your bags? the man said.

Paper bags? Between the sink and the garbage.

He glanced around, then snatched a few bags and shook them open. Into them he loaded the contents of the refrigerator. He picked food off the shelves with both hands, moving fast. When he straightened up, he had it all; every last stick of butter.

He hoisted the bags onto the counter. Plates? he asked. Madeline pointed to the cabinet. He pulled one down, opened the bread, peeled off some turkey loaf, and made a sandwich.

Ugh, Madeline mumbled. I hate turkey loaf.

The man looked at her, half the sandwich in his mouth. With the next bite he took in the rest. His mouth opened so big, it seemed like he could easily toss a few cupcakes in there at the same time. His eyes were blue and glassy. They looked as if they had a film over them, as if he couldn't see out and so she couldn't see in.

This how you do your shopping? Madeline asked.

Lately, he said. He wiped his mouth with his hand and belched.

Madeline could hear Mrs. Lubbock next door. The neighbor had a birdhouse out back and was filling the tray with seed. Every winter bird known to man had gathered somewhere nearby and was chirping like it hadn't eaten since summer.

Then the man started ripping drawers open — silverware, tin foil, pot holders. He pulled them out one by one and left each sagging open like a tongue. When he hit the odds-and-ends drawer, he bent down and scraped through the bulbs and tacks and thread till he grabbed a package of clothesline. He stood up.

What are you doing with that? Madeline asked.

Where's your bedroom? he said.

You wouldn't hurt me, would you? I need to stay healthy for this baby.

He looked past her, as if she was really a shadow behind her. Then he walked toward her and reached over her head for the table. She could smell his body, old sweat and salt, stronger than her own body ever smelled when she lived with the second aunt and had been in the mood to go without washing half a week at a time.

His hand pulled back from the table. He had picked up

179

her scissors and was pointing them at her. Show me your bedroom, he said.

You didn't have a weapon?

I do now.

Madeline shook her head and looked at the floor. She'd let his bark make her think he had a bite. She'd let herself lose her head — and she'd only been inches away from those scissors. Damn. Time to get a grip, girl.

Madeline got off the chair and walked through the living room into the front hallway. By the front door she paused and peered up at the stairs and back toward the living room. From where she stood, everything looked normal. No way of seeing the broken glass or the cut door; they were too far from the front hallway. But she knew everything wasn't normal because she could hear the man behind her, breathing, and in her head she could see those scissors, sharp and gleaming. She walked up the stairs, slowly, and the boards creaked behind her.

At the end of the hall, across from the bathroom — still a little steamy from her hour soak this morning — was Madeline's room. The door was open. Her blanket lay on the floor, and clothes were hanging from the posts and piled all over the dressers. The man looked at her bed, a little twin, and the ice green pillowcases. Nice place, he said. Now, go stand against the bedpost.

He walked up close, pressed his hands to her shoulders, and arranged her so the post went right up against her spine. After sticking the scissors through one of his belt loops, he tore open the clothesline package. He took the middle part of the clothesline, leaving both ends free, and circled the rope around her and the post so she became like a scarecrow with her arms pinned down stiff against her sides. He knotted the rope at her shoulders and her knees, tight enough so she could fall asleep standing up if she wanted. Then he

pushed off his shoes with his feet and tied the loose ends of
the rope to his hands and lay down on the bed, face up to
the ceiling.

Madeline waited a minute for him to say something.
When all he did was swallow and sigh a few times, she said,
Is that what you're doing? You broke in here to take a nap?

He crossed his arms beneath his head and fixed his eyes
on the ceiling. For some of us, he said, it's a luxury.

Sleeping's something everyone's got to do.

If you've got a place to do it in. Some of us aren't always
so lucky. And it's the twentieth of January, you know. Can't
very well sleep along train tracks in the winter. No heat
and no privacy and too much ice left over from that blizzard.
He glanced down from the ceiling and looked at Madeline
with his blank eyes. Turn your head, he said.

Turn it where?

Away.

Madeline looked toward her open door, across the hallway, into the bathroom. The sun lit up the frosted glass of
the window and the jar of bath crystals along the sill. Underneath the tub sat three books. She tried to remember
what was happening in the one she'd shoved back there this
morning. A black-haired French horse breeder had just entered the story.

The man on her bed yawned.

You keep quiet, he said, but if something happens, you
better let me know.

You going to sleep all morning?

I've been wanting a bed for days. I think I'll just see.

Thirteen years that mattress had lain under her body, first
with crib sides and plastic pads for her wetting, then
crowded with dolls until her mother decided Madeline was
getting in the way of romance and sent her to Aunt Number

One, where the dolls were deemed too babylike. Madeline saved some dolls by hiding them in her closet, and at night when the aunt was asleep Madeline pulled the dolls out and curled her arms around them. Aunt Number Two said she didn't mind dolls, and in fact slept with a stuffed rabbit herself, but after Madeline lived there awhile, she brought the dolls, including a twenty-year-old panda that Aunt Number Two had given her, to Goodwill. The aunt cried when Madeline told her, shouting, Now you'll find out what lonely is because you'll have to sleep alone, and tracked down Pop so Madeline could move. That's when Madeline started holding a pillow at night, imagining it was a man sleeping quietly under the covers beside her.

Now, behind her, a man was finally on the bed, his breathing too shallow for him to be asleep. His tossing about made it clear he couldn't settle in. Against the bathroom window the sun had the brightness of late morning, which meant the man had been in the house a few hours. Madeline wiggled her hands, but she couldn't budge them an inch. Next door, Mrs. Lubbock turned on her shower, and the pipes rattled up with water.

The man groaned. Jesus! he said. What the hell's wrong with this mattress? There're all these things sticking into me.

What kinds of things?

Little knots of some kind.

Must be the buttons, Madeline said.

You left the buttons on your mattress? Any lamebrain could tell you you take the buttons off, he said, and flipped himself over.

I never felt them.

It makes no sense to me how you couldn't.

Maybe you just have a sensitive body, Madeline said.

I have slept on rocks, he said. Just yesterday I slept in the weeds by that fence behind your house.

No wonder you came in here looking for a bed.

He didn't say anything. The birds outside kept singing. Madeline tried to sort out the voices. Cardinals, sparrows, chickadees. The man tossed again, muttering a string of curses.

Maybe you should try warm milk, Madeline suggested.

Screw warm milk.

Or relax your tongue. I read that somewhere — you just relax your tongue and everything else follows.

Sure.

Suit yourself.

Outside, Mr. Conover's mutt, Chessie, ran barking through the yards like she always did, and the birds went wild. They flapped up to their hideout under Mrs. Lubbock's eaves and huddled, cooing. For a few mintues, the dog growled and barked at them, then she turned and galloped home, her tags jingling. The birds began squawking and screeching then, chattering like a meeting of angry neighbors. And every peep right next to Madeline's room.

Damn birds! the man said, and leapt out of bed.

Window's already closed, Madeline said, still facing the door.

The curtain hooks squeaked as he drew the curtains shut, but the bird squall sounded as loud as ever. How can you stand this? he said. I thought pigeons were bad. You got any rat poison?

No, Madeline said. Besides, it's not the birds that're bothering you. You're just too wound up. You relax, you'll fall asleep.

I'm relaxed.

Next door, the pipes shuddered as Mrs. Lubbock turned the water off.

Look, Madeline said, why don't you go soak in the tub? That's what I always do.

The man said nothing for a minute. The sparrows' lilting

voices took off and fluttered away, growing dim. Then the chickadees followed. The cardinals held on longer, cheer-cheering softly. Damn birds! the man said again, then banged on the window, and the birds flapped away.

Now everything was quiet. So what do you say? Madeline asked.

The man sighed. Maybe I will. But don't think this means you can get away. I'm keeping you in sight.

Like I can go anywhere.

When the man shuffled into the bathroom he untied the rope from his wrists and knotted the ends to the legs of the tub. Then he stripped off his brown jacket and dumped it on the tile floor. The door was wide open. He turned on the faucet and peeled off his hat and clothes, piling them on the jacket. Everything had a brown tint to it, especially the back of his T-shirt and underwear.

Madeline had never seen what she was seeing at that moment, and it was not what she expected. For one thing, there was so much hair, all over, especially in that place where she had begun to wonder lately if boys had any. For another, his sides were so flat. He looked like a board. But he was all right, except for his skinniness and the scab running down one of his legs, the kind of scab she figured you get from sliding into home plate.

He tested the water with his toe and added more hot.

Try the bath crystals, she told him. They make it much nicer.

He glanced at her, not smiling, and turned and picked through all the shampoo and shaving cream along the sill until he found the crystals. He dumped the whole bottle into the tub and stared at the water. Bubbles crept over the top of the porcelain.

After he climbed in, he lay back, his head resting against the smooth side, his feet perched on the faucet. Ahhh, he said.

Nice, huh, Madeline said.

Where'd you get this stuff?

My boyfriend gave it to me.

Generous guy.

Bathwater splashed a bit and then settled down.

You're on the run, aren't you? she said. You escape from jail?

Never got that far.

How far'd you get?

He sighed and cleared his throat. In a few hours I would've been there. They were getting me ready and then that blizzard blew a tree into the courthouse and the lights went out. That put some serious confusion into the proceedings.

And you escaped.

So to speak.

My boyfriend was in jail.

Which jail?

Some place upstate. I don't remember the name.

What was he in for?

Pulling some guy's arms right out of his sockets.

Why'd he do that?

The guy was calling me names. My boyfriend takes care of me. You got a girlfriend?

So to speak.

She take care of you?

She'd been a real girlfriend, I wouldn't be in this mess.

You loved her?

I would've sold my legs, if it'd have made her happy.

What'd she do — cheat on you?

The man pulled a washcloth off a side hook and soaped it up. You love your boyfriend?

Sure.

He still in jail?

He's getting our house ready. He's coming by for me this afternoon, so I can help him paint.

Well, we'll just take it easy till then.

The sun was gone from the window, so it must have been early afternoon. All Madeline could hear was the man sloshing around. I have this water music, she said. On my tape player. It's real nice.

You stay where you are.

She inched her foot across the carpet and pressed the start button with her big toe. The ocean crashed on the sand, and waves rocked back and forth.

What do you think? Madeline asked.

Nice.

He gave me that too. You know, *From Here to Eternity*.

He takes good care of you. The man swallowed hard. Wish I could say the same for my girl.

I wish you could too, Madeline said.

What're you going to do with me? she asked. The man was standing in front of the bathroom mirror, shaving with Pop's razor. When you leave, that is.

He shook the shaving cream off the razor. Don't ask me.

Well, you look a lot better now, with your hair clean.

Feels better too. He dried off his face with a towel. During the bath he'd opened the window a crack to let out the steam. Now he walked to the window and flung the razor outside.

Shame you've got to put those filthy clothes back on, Madeline said.

No problem, he said. He withdrew the scissors from the pants, tossed the clothes into the tub, bent down, and scrubbed them with the soap. Then he pulled the plug out of the drain, and rinsed the clothes under the faucet. He wrung them out, carried them and the scissors into the bedroom, and lay all that needed to dry on the radiator.

When he turned to her, he was naked and the scissors

were in his hand, pointing down at an angle. Why aren't you scared of me? he said. Aren't you afraid of what I might do?

You seem like a decent enough guy.

He walked over to the bedpost and, still holding the scissors in his hand, untied the knots, working his fingers between the clothesline and Madeline and pushing out until he loosened the rope. The white spiraled to the floor.

I knew a girl like you once, he said.

Did you like her?

She made me laugh.

What happened?

She wasn't smart enough to handle me. She thought she was. She thought she held all the cards. He lay back on the bed and set the scissors beside him, under his hand. I took care of her.

What'd you do?

The man shook his head. She's in her place now.

Even from where Madeline was standing, by the post, she could smell the man. He smelled like peach. She walked around to the bed and sat down by the pillow. Aren't you afraid of what I might do to you? she asked.

He laughed.

Well, aren't you? she said.

He laughed even harder. I'm the one with the scissors, he said. He wrapped his fingers around the blades. Besides, I'm bigger and stronger.

Hand-to-hand combat, I don't stand a chance.

Especially if you want to protect that little baby.

She gave the room a good scan, then stood up and picked her blanket off the floor. She lowered it onto him, from his feet to his head. You go back to sleep, she said.

He kicked the blanket down, so all it came up to were his knees. I don't like to be covered, he said.

Madeline looked him over, from top to bottom and then

all the way back up. His hair was just the right color against the ice green pillows, his skin looked smooth and pink. He closed his eyes and breathed slow and easy.

Every few breaths, he snored. The snoring shook Madeline up the way a fleck of dust on a record shook her up and reminded her that she was listening. He was curled with his knees near his chest, and his hands were balled into fists, and one fist held the scissors. Sometimes the man spoke. Let me in there, he said once. Then, a few minutes later: Perfect. Perfect. What luck.

Later, during a bad dream, when he was shouting so angry she thought he was swearing — only the words were *Mary Jane!* and *Cut it out!* — Madeline lowered her fingers to his head. He was sweating up through his hair. No! he called out, jerking his head as if to throw her off, but she kept holding on and he stayed asleep. Slowly she ran her hand over the crown of his head toward his face, combing his hair. It was damp and fine. There were places where his scalp was tough, and bending closer she could see it was tan there. Maybe a scar.

When she heard the car come to a stop in the driveway, she reached over and tugged on the handle of the scissors. His fingers loosened, and Madeline pulled the weapon away from them. He cleared his throat and moved his tongue around in his mouth and drew his arm to his chest. From him came a mix of peach and sleep. Madeline inhaled. So sweet and lovely. She tucked the scissors under the mattress where she was sitting and leaned back. Downstairs the front door slammed shut, and Madeline gazed toward her open bedroom door.

Her pop made right for the stairway. His footsteps were heavy enough on the stairs to wake the dead, but her visitor slept on, and Madeline was not going to wake him. At the top of the stairs Pop called out, Where are you, honey? You taking a bath? He trudged down the hall and paused just before he reached her room. Then he stepped into her doorway. Madeline was sitting on the bed, her arm resting on the shoulder of a naked man.

Who's this? her pop said, pointing.

The man rustled and his fingers came out of their fists.

Pop stepped closer. Who's this man here? he asked.

The man rolled onto his back and looked up into her father's eyes.

Pop, Madeline said, this here's the daddy.

What? the man said, still groggy. He rubbed his eyes.

Pop, he came here to propose to me. He's come to be with me. He's come here to stay.

The man was looking right at Madeline. It seemed as though the film had finally come off his eyes, so he saw her at last, and she felt as if she could finally see him — or she would, once she cut through his glazed look of shock.

SINCE NANNA
CAME TO STAY

"LOOK AT THE FLOOR," Nanna said to Beth, pointing through the legs of party guests which seemed to the two of them, low to the linoleum as they were, like beach pillars planted exactly where they would block the view. Beth, six years old, stood next to her grandmother, who sat ankles crossed and alert on her favorite chair beside the stove. She peered through the spaces between the stockinged and trousered legs. "From this angle," Nanna whispered, "you can see right through the floor — the way you can see through glass if you shade your eyes at night." She lifted her wrinkled hand, dazzling with all her rings, and squinted as if she were looking for a ship. "And if you stand just right you can see all your father's girlfriends swimming around under the floor. See?"

Beth leaned against the webbed beach chair — the chair Nanna carried on walks, to the mall, the supermarket, and now into the kitchen at Beth's parents' party — shielded her eyes from the fluorescent light of the kitchen, and scanned the room. Nanna was tinier than any lady Beth had met before, and the seat of her chair was only a few inches from the floor, so when Beth stood beside her seated grandmother at this party, their eyes looked out to the world at precisely the same level. And of course Beth would stand beside Nanna here. For the past six months, Beth had stood beside Nanna everywhere.

"Aren't they beautiful?" Nanna said, smiling at the scene under the tiles.

"I'm not sure I see them."

Nanna pointed. "I think that one is the sweetest. Such black hair. And so long. But all their hair is long, isn't it. Richard always did like it down to the waist."

Beth tilted her head this way and that, her own hair brushing the bow on her back. She wiped her bangs from her eyes as she strained to make out the women in the floor. There were Mrs. Wilson's black heels and Mr. Ahern's brown loafers and Miss Candlebury's sandals. And the white floor underneath. "I can't see them, Nanna."

"But there they are, half a dozen, clear as day. And their hair, billowing around them like sea flowers. Such lovely creatures. That was always the case with your father. Martin had good sense and endless creativity, but Richard was so traditional. Men had to be men and women women. I'm still surprised he lets your mother work."

Beth thought she made out the crest of a blond head, but it turned out to be a fallen potato puff. "Nanna, why would Daddy's girlfriends be in the floor?" she asked.

"Because," Nanna said, resting her hand on Beth's organdy sleeve, "he has to stash them somewhere, hasn't he?"

Beth hadn't known that her father had girlfriends, or that girlfriends were even something daddies had. But if Beth could have girlfriends, then she supposed her father could have girlfriends as well, and they would have to live somewhere. "I guess so." Beth bit into a cube of cheese. It had a funny taste that reminded her of pigs, which she no longer ate since Nanna told her about a pet pig, now buried in Uncle Martin's yard. Beth stretched her mouth into a grimace but swallowed anyway.

"If you don't like it," Nanna said, extracting the rest of the cheese from Beth's hand, "get rid of it." She glanced beyond Beth's side toward the living room, then flung the cheese in the opposite direction, behind the stove. It had good company there: the tasteless morsels ("That's all they have at this shindig — morsels!") from tonight, plus all the pills she'd asked Beth to hide since she'd moved in.

She turned to Beth, grinning. Beth always thought of Nanna's face as being like the masks her parents had on the living room wall. She couldn't read yet, but they'd told her the names: Comedy and Tragedy. Nanna's face was doughy, with all kind of folds, and it was always Comedy or Tragedy, the only exception being when Nanna was asleep, and then it was just one big open mouth, sucking in the air as if it were a sinkhole.

Richard came into the kitchen then. Nanna and Beth recognized him by the cuff of his trousers. Richard always wore nice clothes. These pants had lines on them which reminded Beth of long, skinny combs, Nanna of rake marks in the dirt, and Marie — Beth's mother — of an accountant. They heard what Marie thought before the party, when she and Richard were fixing up the living room and Nanna and Beth were in the kitchen, discussing the best place to set up Nanna's chair. "Shh," Nanna said, a vertical rubied finger to her lips, then to Beth's. "But I *am* an accountant," Richard said.

"You don't have to look it every minute of the day," Marie said. "If you considered wearing something else, it might help separate you from the office."

"Don't remind me of the office," Richard said. "I've seen little glitches in the books before but never a hole the size of Cincinnati." He carried a bowl of stuffed mushrooms toward the kitchen but stopped short in the archway. "Mother, what is Beth doing with that umbrella?"

Nanna and Beth had set up beside the stove, and Beth

was screwing a pink beach umbrella to the back of the folding chair. "I would do it, Richy, but, you know, my hands . . ." Nanna held up the ringed fingers that after bedtime in the moonlight she and Beth agreed resembled miniature trees.

"You cannot have an umbrella on your chair at this party," Richard said.

"But it's a beach party, Daddy."

"No," Richard said. "It's a bon voyage party. A have-a-good-vacation party."

"Point Pleasant is a beach," Nanna said. Then with one hand she swept her bifocals into her lap while with the other she slipped on a pair of purple sunglasses. She crossed her arms against her chest. Richard stared fiercely at her for a minute, then shuffled out of the room.

Now Nanna and Beth had been huddled beneath the umbrella all night. Beth wore her star-shaped sunglasses, though to see what Nanna saw in the floor she had pushed them to the top of her head. Wally, Richard's boss, kept bringing them foaming drinks, and they rested the Hawaiian god mugs along the armrest of the chair, sipping from time to time. A few guests — Richard's business associates, Marie's coworkers at the clothing store — came up to say hello, but because the Nanna and Beth party was a crouch too low for everyone except Nanna and Beth, no one stayed very long. Which gave Nanna and Beth complete freedom to talk about people, something Nanna dearly loved to do.

As they watched Richard stride through the crowd, across the kitchen, Beth noted how men parted, almost bowing, to let him through. "He's the king!" she said. Her father walked briskly, his bald head gleaming as if he wore a cap of light. "You think so?" Nanna said. "I don't know . . ." But then Nanna's attention was caught by a skinny woman with a long neck. "Doesn't she look like a crane?" Nanna said. "Except for the nose," Beth said. (Nanna had shown

196

her pictures of cranes in a book.) "It's not long enough." Nanna contemplated the profile while Beth nibbled on a pastry. "Yes, I see what you mean. Now over there" — she pointed to a beak-nosed man eating crackers across the room — "I'll bet he gets invited to banquets in bird sanctuaries for Thanksgiving." "Yeah," Beth said.

In the corner, Richard had settled onto a breakfast stool, where he was talking to Charles, his best friend from work. Richard was saying something Beth could barely hear, but with such force that his head bobbed forward with each word, and Charles kept wiping his face with his hand as if he had a rash over his mouth. When Richard paused, Charles asked a question that began with the sound *ex,* and Richard nodded, eyes down.

Nanna's gaze meandered once the birdman migrated from the room. "Oh, look," Nanna said, directing with her chin.

Beth followed the chin to the floor below her father's chair. The light glared terribly. "What do you see, Nanna?"

Nanna slurped the bottom of her drink. "All his girlfriends have swum up beneath him. They've gathered by his chair, and their little fins are flicking back and forth."

Beth stretched her neck to see beyond the glare. "Come here," Nanna said, hooking her finger. Beth moved so that she was almost cheek to cheek with Nanna, and so close she felt enveloped by Nanna's honeysuckle. Nanna pointed her finger like a telescope, right above Beth's cheekbone. Beth closed one eye and looked. The glare cleared, and yes, beneath the floor Beth saw the flowing hair, as long as her mother's; the diaphanous dresses; the school of mermaids with slender, paddling tails. "Ooh," she said, as Nanna lowered her head into the starting position for a nod. "I see them."

Upstairs, in their room after the party, Beth unzipped Nanna's girdle. There were still a few guests below, but Nanna

197

and Beth had tired of the floor and the boring talk around them ("Sounds like the TV when it's just dots," Beth had said, referring to the time that she and Nanna, unable to sleep, had sneaked downstairs and discovered to their dismay nothing but snow on the television), and besides, they couldn't find Wally to make any more drinks. So they had picked up the chair and told Richard and Marie good night.

Before Nanna moved into this house, Beth's mother had said, "What are we going to do?" There was one extra bedroom, but Richard had recently begun working there late into the night, staring at papers with little boxes and numbers so small that Beth didn't understand how anyone could see them. At Uncle Martin's, Nanna had had her own room, but last winter Uncle Martin went to teach children on a mountain somewhere and Nanna's lungs proved too old to get her up the steep trails, so she was going to have to stay with Beth's family until the end of the summer.

All this Beth heard while she sat at the top of the stairs, listening. "Why can't we just put your mother someplace, like other families do?" "You think we have that kind of money to spare? Money's why we haven't gone to see her for years." "That's not why we haven't gone to see her. We haven't gone to see her because you're her unfavorite son." "I don't want to get into that now." "All I know is, I don't want to take care of her, Richard. Martin says she's past her prime." "He didn't mean she was incapacitated. He just meant she's an exaggeration of what she once was." "And you want to subject yourself to that?" "No. But the bottom line is, I'll feel bad if we don't let her stay here. She's my mother, Marie."

The first night, Beth opened the sofa downstairs. She liked how that felt: she pulled and pulled and just when she didn't expect it, the frame rose up in her hands like a jaw opening suddenly, and then she had to run away or it might bite down onto her. Beth also helped Marie with the sheets, which was no fun at all because the mattress was rounded and the sheets square. The whole time her mother kept saying, "Your grandmother is a character. Remember how you liked her?" though when Beth last saw Nanna, her grandmother was just another skirt outside the crib bars.

And then Nanna stepped into the house. She wore a dress with blue butterflies and a necklace of white beads and at least one ring on every finger. She closed her eyes as she walked through the door and when satisfied that she was inside, drew a deep breath and said, "Beth." Over her head Richard pressed his fingers toward Marie, mouthing, "Eight bags." "Welcome, Harriet," Marie said, walking close and hugging Nanna. Then she and Richard went to the car, and Nanna crouched down and held her arms out. Beth stepped slowly across the room, and when the arms closed around her they reminded her of the caves she sometimes built with chairs and old suitcases. But Nanna's arms were softer than a cave, and smelled like honeysuckle. "Your eyes have little birds in them," Nanna said as Beth pulled her face back. With her right hand she reached toward Beth's eyes and snatched at the air. Then she turned her hand over and brought it between them. Beth watched closely as Nanna uncurled her fingers, but she must not have been quick enough; Nanna's hand was empty. "Oh dear," Nanna said, her eyes darting around the room, her face drooping into Tragedy. "They flew away."

The music from the party — too new for Nanna, too old for Beth — clicked off downstairs. Beth held up her arms, and Nanna raised the organdy dress over her head. "Could you believe that Wally Robertson?" Nanna said. "Yelling at Charles in the corner like that. Whatever Charles told him certainly made Wally one angry man." She laid the dress over the back of the chair, on top of her own clothes. "The last time I heard such talk was when I lived in Istanbul. Did I ever tell you about Turkey?"

"You told me about the city that looked like sand castles."

"I did? I wonder where that was. Well, in Istanbul, the air was full of espionage, intrigue, betrayal. I once saw two men dueling with swords on the edge of the Grand Bazaar. Nepal was a breeze compared to that."

While Beth pulled on her father's T-shirt and Nanna slipped on a nightie, Beth tried to imagine what these places with such funny names looked like, but they all merged into one big darkness, somewhere out there. Nanna flopped on her bed, and Beth did the same on hers, and they lay on their stomachs, resting their chins on their arms, and their arms on the long windowsill. The window was open and air was blowing in lightly, just enough to ripple the clothes on their backs. Above the trees — silhouettes now, the leaves at the bottom laced with white from the lantern by the front door — stars blinked across the sky.

"Did you know there are pictures in the stars, Nanna? Daddy told me so." He did this when Beth was much younger: held her in his arms in the backyard, pointed up, and called out the picture names. Beth liked this game, but with him always working late in the extra room, it had been a long time since he'd said yes when she'd asked him to play.

"That's what people did for TV before there was TV," Nanna said. "Just like you do with clouds."

Beth looked into the sky. It didn't take much to make out a woman in a rocking chair, or a ballerina, but she didn't think these were the same things that her father had said he could see in the sky. Beth explained this to Nanna.

Nanna replied, "You see, the sky is God's sheet when He goes to bed at night, but it's a sheet with holes in it. The stars are those holes and what you're seeing through them is God Himself in bed. That's why the pictures look different every night; sometimes God doesn't tuck His sheet in properly, so things get shifted around a little."

Outside, Richard and Marie were seeing off some guests. Marie stood by the curb, saying bye to a car of her friends. Richard stood in the driveway, talking low to Charles. Their heads were bowed together, and Richard was running his hands through his hair.

"Your father and Charles, they speak their own language together," Nanna said.

Beth listened hard and it was true, she couldn't make out anything they were saying. Might as well have been bees buzzing far away. "Can you understand them, Nanna?" she asked.

"Goodness, no," Nanna said, pulling down the shade and rolling onto her back. "I have never understood your father."

The next morning when they came down for breakfast, Richard was on the phone, trailing the cord through the kitchen archway into the living room. Marie was drinking a cup of coffee in the kitchen. Beth and Nanna sat at the table and poured themselves the cereal that Marie had left out.

"Can't believe I have to go to work," Marie said. "Throw a party two nights before we leave, then put off getting anything ready till the last possible day. I must be out of my mind. Think you two could start packing before I get home?"

Nanna said of course. Marie set her cup down on the kitchen counter and walked into the living room. "There's cleaning up and having our mail held for three weeks." She came back in, arms full of Hawaiian mugs and beer bottles.

"Calling the newspaper, picking up the dry cleaning." She glanced at them. "And Beth, those bangs have got to go." She downed the last of her coffee just as Richard rounded the corner and hung up the phone, saying, "Charles called him after the party and laid all the cards on the table."

Marie blew air out in a stream. "That wasn't too smart," she said.

"I told him I wanted to get the paperwork together and report it first. I told him you can never be sure how people will act when they're confronted. But he got drunk and lost his head and now Wally knows that we know, and, oh, God . . ."

The two of them talked, and Nanna and Beth watched. Marie stood close to Richard, the look on her face the same soft look she sometimes had when hugging him. Richard kept pressing the skin on his forehead in small circles. "I'm sure I don't have to worry," he mumbled. "Wally's the guy who did something illegal, not me."

"He's a powerful man," Marie said, shaking her head. "And arrogant enough to help himself to company money."

"But what can he do to me? I have a contract you couldn't break with a battery of lawyers."

"I know," Marie said, sighing. "I know."

Beth looked away from them to her cereal sponging up the milk. Nanna's first morning here, she told Marie to go on to work, not to concern herself with Beth's breakfast. Beth remembered it, Nanna setting the table with the silverware upside down ("Well, what end should face your mouth? Surely not the handle") and whipping up scrambled eggs that they had colored purple. The dye came from a jar in one of Nanna's bags; one tiny drop and the yellow in the pan turned purple, as quick as a storm cloud could turn a day dark. Now, Beth dragged her spoon in figure eights around the bowl while her parents droned on.

Richard's kiss on top of her head came suddenly; his skin was as hot as a fever. "Vacation's tomorrow, right?" he said. "Right!" Beth replied in her best voice. He stepped toward the back door, saying, "I'll blow up the inner tube and take you out in the waves, just you and me, like we did last summer." For a moment he seemed almost happy, the way he used to be before all his late-night working, but as Marie followed him into the garage and the engine revved up, Beth felt two wet imprints in the shape of her father's hands cooling on her shoulders. She and Nanna watched as the car pulled down the street, and when it rounded the corner, Nanna turned to Beth, clasping her hands together. "Time for an excursion!" she said.

They dumped their mushy cereal in the trash and helped themselves to the leftover candy kisses. Then they dressed and left the house, Nanna holding the beach chair with one hand and Beth with the other. It was a clear, sunny day, and felt nowhere near as deep into summer as it actually was. A nice breeze played around the trees, and roses bloomed in neighbors' gardens. They walked slowly, talking, and every ten minutes or so Nanna grew hot or tired, and they had to stop so she could sit in her chair. Beth climbed into her lap then, and they waved at the cars that passed by and watched high school boys mowing people's lawns. The sitting was as much fun as the walking, so a few times they watched as whole lawns got mowed while they chatted. During one such rest, Beth asked Nanna what Richard had been like when he was a little boy.

Nanna paused a minute. "He always thought we didn't have enough," she said finally. "Martin was so much easier; things concerned him as little as they concerned me. This is what I tried to teach Richy. But he was so fussy. He hated that I wore fake jewels." She looked at her hands. "Wouldn't come with me when I said the heck with stability and took my savings and went to live in Europe. I told Richard it would break the family apart if he didn't come, but he wouldn't give up his little security, said he wanted to live a *normal* life when he grew up so it was more important that he keep making money then. Working in a grocery store was more important? He was still a baby."

Beth had heard about this store, the grocers with pencils behind their ears, the belts carrying boxes up in the middle of the detergent aisle. She imagined her father there as a baby — What had he looked like then? Was he chubby? Had he always been bald, with no more than a smudge of hair around the back of his head? Beth tried to see him in diapers, waddling through the supermarket aisles, pointing confused shoppers to the tomato paste, leading lost children back to their mothers. She knew that he could have run the whole place, even with a pacifier in his mouth. Her mind came back to Nanna as Nanna was saying, ". . . and wouldn't come to Greece that time I got sick, though Martin *begged* him. One excuse after another."

"What?" Beth said.

Nanna paused, as if forgetting what she was saying. "Oh, did you hear that? The cars up there are calling to us."

Beth glanced in the direction of Nanna's gaze. Yes, she could hear the cars, speeding along the busy road beyond the houses. "That's the big street, and I'm not allowed to cross it."

"I won't make you cross it. Hop down, now."

Together they wound their way out of the neighborhood and when they reached the big road, they walked along it, not across. They passed the church and the gas station, then walked by the ugly buildings where Nanna said doctors must work, and the smelly place where buses seemed to live, and then they came to a little mall. Here they peered into all the windows, "Just to see what they have," Nanna said. There was a deli, where Nanna bought Beth a green ice pop (exactly the kind of food Beth's mother would never allow in the house, and oh, it tasted so good!), and a shoe store with silver pumps that glittered, and a drugstore, where the girl behind the counter had a mustache — from suppressing belches, Nanna explained, it has to come out somehow — and finally a barbershop. Nanna spoke for a while to the barber, a tall man with a white apron and as little hair on his head as Beth's father. Beth was still sucking on the green ice pop when the barber asked her if she wanted the regular chair — "It does go up and down," he noted — or the chair that looked like a car. Naturally she chose the car, though she was disappointed to realize, as he lowered her into it and Nanna set her own chair down across the room by the window, that the car was only a metal frame around a regular chair and it didn't even go up and down. The barber took the plastic tubing from the ice pop away, and snip snip went his scissors. Nanna waved to Beth in the car, and Beth steered an invisible wheel, pretending she really thought it was a car so Nanna would not be as disappointed as she was, all the time wishing the wheel would become real in her hands and the car real around her body, the same way that the floor at the party had become a pool of women. But without Nanna at her side the car was clearly no more than a chair, and Beth's brown curls fell to the floor. When they walked out into the sun, the air licked the back of Beth's neck and her face felt larger than ever before. "You look lovely," Nanna said, turning Beth toward her reflection in the plate glass.

But after they found their way home, there was Beth's mother, staring at Beth as she and Nanna strolled hand in hand up the front walk. Actually, she was not staring at Beth as much as at her head, and then she was staring at Nanna, and her mother's face looked as if at any minute it would turn into the scowl of the Hawaiian god mug.

"How could you!" Marie yelled at Nanna after she sent

Beth to her room and Beth nestled into the corner at the top of the stairs, watching through the bannister.

"You said she needed a haircut." Nanna covered her mouth and looked at the floor beyond Marie's feet.

"But not a *crew cut*. Do you think this is how little girls are supposed to look?"

"I don't know. I thought she looked nice."

"It is not at all what I had in mind. And Richard will be devastated. You know how he loved her hair. I hadn't cut it in two years."

"I'm sorry, Marie."

"Well, there's nothing we can do about it now." Marie sat down with a thud on the living room sofa.

"You said —"

"I know what I said. I know what I said, and let's just drop it." Marie twirled a tassel from a pillow. The fringe opened like a white dandelion. Marie looked toward the front window and sighed long and loud. "It's just with all that's going on right now. And on top of everything, we're leaving on this trip."

Nanna stood up. "We will pack. Right now. We'll fill up those suitcases, and then you'll have one less thing to worry about."

Marie's gaze lingered out the window for a minute. Then she turned to Nanna as slowly as smoke unfurling. "Excuse me?" she said. "Did you say something?"

Nanna had moved into Beth's room because the two of them were together so much anyway, it just made more sense than tripping over the convertible sofa in the living room all the time. Nanna did not mind. Neither did Beth. Once their beds were in the same room, they could stay awake talking for hours until one of them fell asleep. There was so much to say — people to whisper about, Nanna's memories to laugh at, things to see in the ceiling.

On clear nights, the light coming through the window made Nanna's rings reflect colors onto the ceiling. Reds and greens and blues swirled above them. "Make them chase each other, Nanna," Beth said this night as the phone rang below. "Goodness," Nanna replied, hunting her left hand after her right. "Where did you get such a mean streak?"

Right hand hid in the corner. Left hand found it and pounced. "I don't know," Beth said, giggling. The red stones closed over the green and blue.

It was still dark when Richard came in to wake them up. He shook Nanna first. "What?" she said.

"We're going to get an early start," Richard said, stepping over to Beth.

"But you said eight o'clock. You said eight."

"I haven't been able to sleep all night."

"Can't you have a little patience? How can we get ready in the dark?"

"Look, I'm sorry, but things are getting weird, and I want to hit the road before the office opens and I get sucked back into it."

In the bathroom — Nanna left the lights off and the curtains closed so their eyes wouldn't "sting from the light"— Nanna soaped up Beth's hair while her own hair set in hot curlers. "Your father is always running," she said. "When he was in grade school, every day he left an hour before your Uncle Martin and all the other children just to be first in line to walk into the building. He used to arrive before the janitor! I would say, 'Richy, enjoy life, smell the roses,' but he would not listen to me. How did he get to be like that? Certainly not from the genes. His father never even stayed in one family, let alone one job. And I have always regarded institutional loyalty as the outgrowth of a fearful and therefore conformist mind."

Nanna kept talking, but the soap was in Beth's eyes so

207

she dunked her head beneath the water. There, surrounded by the muffled sounds of bath and Nanna, Beth wondered for the first time how her father's girlfriends got into the floor. Maybe it was by way of the tub, the same tub she was in now. Maybe they lay in the water and when the plug came out they slid through the drain, into the walls of the house, and downstairs to a lake under the kitchen floor. Beth almost asked Nanna to help her try this, but they were in such a hurry. Instead she figured she'd ask when they got back home. Nanna could pull the plug and watch over Beth. Nanna would make sure everything was OK.

Richard drove. Marie sat beside him, and Nanna sat behind him, and Beth sat next to Nanna. Nanna bought a box of funny newspaper articles she had collected over the years, but when she pulled them out to look at, she felt too queasy — Richard was driving like a demon, she said, and the roads were so very bumpy. She held her hand over her stomach and belched. Beth laughed. Richard said, "Please, Mother." Marie held her head in her hands.

Then it was highway and an occasional traffic light, but mostly it was nothing else. No windowless buildings, no trains clattering beside them, no billboards even. Just trees. "And green is a pretty boring color," Nanna pointed out to Beth, "if you're honest about it." Beth stopped looking outside after the first half hour, and she and Nanna tried to get something interesting going, but there wasn't much they could latch onto. "You poor thing," Nanna whispered as they passed a lake. "When we went on trips I always had them singing. Well, Martin, anyway. Your father could not carry a tune, or at least said he couldn't."

At that, Nanna glanced up, to the back of Richard's bald head. She started, then said softly, "Take a peek up there." They were sitting low in the seat and Nanna was pointing.

"Your father has a face on the back of his head. See? There's the mouth and the nose and the eyes." She traced the face in the air with her finger, mouth being where the spine hit the neck, nose a fat fold above that, eyes two slitted dimples that made the face look Asian.

"Hey," Beth said, "that's neat."

"What's neat?" Richard called out from the front.

Nanna said, "The little house I just made with my hands."

Beth giggled and watched the face with Nanna as they drove. If her father turned right, the face turned left. He glanced up, and the face squished into a frown. Nanna played along with it. When a car cut in front of them and Richard swore, the face looked to be smiling, and Nanna whispered, "Have a nice day." When Richard smoked a cigarette — "Daddy, I thought you quit," Beth said, to which he replied, "I need something to unwind" — and tossed the butt out the window, the face scrunched up on one side, and Nanna said, "Tsk, tsk." Every time, she and Beth got a good laugh going.

Then Richard pulled into a rest stop. "You two go take a break," he said, "I've got to give Charles a call. I'm worried about him."

In the bathroom, Nanna waited while Beth used the toilet all by herself. When she came out, and Nanna was combing her crew cut, Beth said, "How'd Daddy get that face?"

"He was born with it," Nanna said.

"Are we all born with two faces?"

Nanna paused to slip the comb into her purse. "Yes," she said. "Your father's is just more obvious."

Back in the car, out on the road, Nanna found a pack of cards and she and Beth began a game of Go Fish. Richard and Marie talked adult talk — Marie spoke of "poor Charles," and Richard said "Wally's threats are idle," and then they began with big words like "he's defending through offensive," and Beth stopped listening. Fortunately, Nanna had overcome her motion sickness, so she and Beth had no trouble playing cards. The sun shone through the window, and Beth could barely see out, but at some point she glanced up, squinting, and noticed a yellow light changing to red, and heard her father muttering, "Oh well, too late," as they coasted through an intersection. A minute passed, and her parents continued with their talk. Soon the road opened out to fields, and Beth grew bored with the game. "Do you know where the king, queen, and jack come from?" Nanna said, gathering up the cards, and as she was explaining that cards were once used for money by rival kingdoms, a police car with flashing lights sped up behind them on the highway and pulled them over.

"It was yellow when I started going through, wasn't it?" Richard mumbled in the front seat while the officer sidled up to their car.

From where Beth sat she couldn't see the man's face but she could see his creaseless uniform and shiny boots and she could hear his voice, asking for her father's license. "This is so embarrassing," Richard said, glancing at the cars passing by as the officer walked ahead to his car and spoke into his car radio. "And now the insurance will go up . . ." He tilted his head back and took a deep breath, and the second face squeezed together as if puckering from the sourness of the situation.

It seemed like a whole day passed before the officer set his radio back in his car. "I don't see a ticket. Maybe he let you off," Marie said as the man approached. But he didn't let Richard off. Instead, he walked up to Richard's window and said, "I'd like you to step out of the car, sir."

"Excuse me?" Richard said.

"Speeding," Nanna whispered to Beth, but then the officer said, "We have a warrant out for you."

Marie rustled suddenly, as if she had just dropped something.

"Is this about my office?" Richard said. "I haven't done anything. All I've done is uncover stuff."

He talked on, and as he did the face on the back of his head grinned, and the eyes squinted with glee. To Beth, it seemed to be saying, I stole the cookies and I'm getting away with it, and after she watched for a minute she couldn't help herself. "He did it!" she squealed.

Richard reeled around. "What are you doing?" he said, looking paler and more scared than she had ever seen.

"Please step out of the car," the officer said. Richard opened the door slowly. The face winked at Nanna and Beth as Richard's feet touched down on the road and when he stood up beside the car, he was saying, "He's framing me, and now no one will believe me."

The policeman slammed the door then, and Marie spun around, facing Beth, and her eyes were wide and wet and seemed to bulge out of her head. "Why did you say that?" Marie screamed. "Beth! What has gotten into you?"

Beth almost felt herself begin to cry, but instead she swallowed hard, and the cry went away, and she answered with the only thought that came to mind. "I didn't say anything. My other face said it."

"What?" Marie glanced at Nanna.

Nanna looked down, grinning, knitting her hands together.

"What is going on?" Marie yelled. She brushed a sheet of tears and sweat off her cheeks. Her brow was furrowed and she looked sick. "What is Beth talking about?"

Nanna opened her mouth as if to speak and then she stopped and peered up, through the front windshield. Beth rose on her knees to see. Beside the police car, the officer was snapping handcuffs on Richard's wrists. Beth could see nothing but her father's profile; she could not see either face. "Look," she said, and her mother whirled around. "It's a lie!" her mother shrieked, wrenching open the door and bolting toward the police car. Beth turned to Nanna as her mother ran across the gravel. For the first time, the old woman's face was neither Comedy nor Tragedy. She was simply watching calmly, not saying anything, so Beth knew that it had to be true.